C000133268

# The Knight With 1,000 Eyes

Book III of the Galhadrian Trilogy

Jan-Andrew Henderson

Black Hart Entertainment

Edinburgh. Brisbane.

Published by Black Hart, Edinburgh 2021
Black Hart Entertainment.
32 Glencoul Ave, Dalgetty Bay, Fife KY11 9XL.

The rights of the author to be identified as the author of this work
has been ascertained in accordance with the Copyrights, Designs
and Patents Act 1988.

All rights reserved. No part of this publication may be reproduced,
distributed or transmitted in any form or by any means without
prior written permission.
-
Publisher's Note: This is a work of fiction. Names, characters,
places, and incidents are a product of the authors' imagination. Locales and public names are sometimes used for atmospheric
purposes. Any resemblance to actual people, living or dead, or to
businesses, companies, events, institutions, or locales is completely
coincidental.

Cover by Panagiotis Lampridis (BookDesignStars)
Book Layout © 2017 BookDesignTemplates.com

**The Knight With 1,000 Eyes**.
978-1-64826-886-1
978-1-63625-841-6 eBook

# Praise for the Galhadrian Trilogy

A great read. I couldn't put it down - *Teen Titles*

Gripping from page one. Timeless - *Write Away!*

A cracking read - *The Sunday Post*

Fast, furious and gripping - *The School Librarian*

Skilful and well-paced - *Scottish Association of Teachers*

Enough plot to power half a library - *Scotsman Newspaper*

A winner. This book has it all' - *Derby Telegraph*

Thrilling - *Newsround, BBC TV*

Appealing and authentic - *Sunday Herald*

A guaranteed bestseller - *The Afternoon Show*

Action packed and highly imaginative - *Bookfest*

Fast moving & inventive - *Scottish Book Collector*

*Some folklorists believe that King Arthur once lived and fought in Scotland... Possibly he was a Celtic Cavalry leader with a swift-moving force.*

Raymond Lamont-Brown. *Scottish Folklore.*

For Scarlet

# Chapters

# Part 1

*And so there grew great tracts of wilderness,*

*Wherein the beast was ever more and more,*

*But man was less and less, till Arthur came.*

Alfred, Lord Tennyson. *Idylls of the King.*

A small group got off the Edinburgh to Inverness express and huddled on the platform, waiting for the train to Wick. There were only a few people around, which was probably a good thing, as they wanted to stay hidden. Anyone who spotted them usually circled round for another look at the Clan, as they called themselves.

Small wonder. Shadowjack Henry was a giant of a man while Uallabh, dressed in black leather, looked like a cross between a wild west gunslinger and a vampire. Peazle wore a bowler hat and brightly patterned waistcoat. Duncan had a thick black mane, almost covering his shoulders. Only Charlie and Lilly seemed normal.

They were all on a secret mission. To deliver a magical wooden cup, the Grail, to Lilly's father - the mighty wizard, Gorrodin.

They had plenty of reason to be cautious. The group were being hunted by dark creatures, controlled by Lilly's mother, Morgana. Morgana was preparing to go to war with Galhadria, and the Grail would secure her a swift victory. The Lords of the Western Wilderness, guardians of Galhadria, expected the Clan to take the cup to Wick and deliver it to them through a 'thin place' - one of the magical portals to Galhadria. When the Lords found out they were being double-crossed, their retribution would be terrible.

The Clan didn't know it yet, but someone else was looking for them. Police Inspector Archer was on their trail, for he had promised Charlie's parents he would find their missing son.

# The Clan

Inspector Archer stood at the entrance to Waverly Station, staring up at the famous towering silhouette that was Edinburgh's Old Town. Crowds of shoppers surged in and out of the stores lining Princes Street, fat plastic bags of shopping clunking against each other. They hardly glanced at the tall, bald man in a suit and tie, raincoat draped over one arm, gawping like a tourist. The castle rose above the bustling thoroughfare, as it had done for a thousand years, ancient and serene.

Archer turned to a uniformed policeman strolling past.

"Could you tell me the way to the nearest station officer?"

"It's about ten feet behind you, sir. You just came out of it."

"Not the train station." Inspector Archer pulled out a worn brown wallet with a gold badge inside. "The nearest police station."

The locomotive to Wick was an asthmatic old diesel, chugging sluggishly through the mountain passes of the Scottish highlands, pulling three dingy carriages. Even in the 21st century, there were few people living in the far north, so transport to and from remote areas was infrequent and poorly maintained. Since it was a weekday, the only other occupants of the carriage, apart from the Clan, were an old man in a flat cap and a stout woman wearing a large tweed coat, accompanied by a young boy and girl. The mother was absorbed in some glossy magazine and occasionally passed a soggy, homemade sandwich to her offspring. Both children sat with their foreheads flat against the greasy carriage window, chewing placidly and watching grazing cattle glide past.

"How much farther now?" Shadowjack yawned loudly, stretching huge muscular arms, which almost spanned the breadth of the carriage.

"Where are ye headed, son?" The old man doffed his cap. He wore an olive Barbour jacket and green Wellingtons - a postcard-perfect picture of an elderly countryman.

"Someplace called Lairg," Shadowjack replied.

"It's the next stop, but we're still twenty-odd miles away." The old man jerked his thumb towards the window. "This is the Pass of Shin."

The giant leaned across him and looked out, then withdrew his head sharply. The train was winding its way along a narrow ledge not much wider than the locomotive itself. A few feet beyond, the ground sheared away, dropping through a chaotic mass of trees to a dark, frothing river.

"Name's Paul Jessop, by the way," the old man said amiably.

"Shadowjack Henry."

"Sounds foreign."

"I was born just outside Glasgow."

"Aye. Foreign." Paul Jessop said with a knowing smirk. "Born and bred in the north myself. Never got off in Lairg, though. Bit too cosmopolitan for my liking." He gave the blacksmith a jokey wink. "It's got a visitor centre *and* a caravan site."

Shadowjack nodded politely, then pretended to go to sleep.

Charlie Wilson had a seat to himself. Uallabh and Peazle were sitting together on the other side of the aisle, both engrossed in their own thoughts. Duncan and Lilly were in front of him, talking to each other in low tones, while Shadowjack was beyond them - he was so big, he needed two seats for himself.

It was the first time since this insane adventure had begun that Charlie had time to think properly about his situation - and wasn't sure he wanted to.

He was worried about his mum and dad. They must be frantic by now, wondering where he was. And he was terrified of what might happen next. He had almost died twice already, and who knew what dangers were still waiting for him?

And, looking at Lilly and Duncan together, he realised he was jealous. Lilly was laughing at something Duncan had just said, and Charlie could smell the faint freshness of her red curls bobbing above the seat back. The highlander might seem gruff and serious, but he was also smart and brave - as well as being two hundred years closer to Lilly's age than Charlie. The boy had to keep reminding himself that Lilly was as ancient as the hills they were passing - and only half-human. She looked so young and so... pretty.

There was no point in fooling himself. He was no more than a child to her. Twice now, Lilly had manipulated him into some suicidal scheme to further her aims. As he well knew, Galhadrians weren't big on gratitude. Yet he would continue to help the girl, if only because he felt it was the right thing to do.

He looked around at his companions - marvelling at what a mixed bunch they were. Why were they all participating in this crazy adventure? Lilly had an obvious reason - she wanted to free her father, trapped in a mountain cave. But the rest had little to gain. Duncan had been forced to abandon his all-consuming search for his brother. Peazle was betraying his own master,. Jack Thane. He would, doubtless, be punished for his treachery, if Thane were as callous as he seemed. Shadowjack had given up the peaceful life on his forge to lend assistance - though he had never met Lilly before. And Uallabh seemed to hold no love for humans or Galhadrians, yet had come along too.

There seemed to be only one plausible reason for everyone's folly.

They were lonely. He, Lilly, Peazle, Duncan, Uallabh and even Shadowjack Henry.

Now they had each other. Each time they risked their lives for their companions, the bonds between them grew stronger. Charlie glanced over at Uallabh, sitting tense as a statue on the other side of the aisle. An overhanging branch slapped the side of the train, and the warrior jumped, hand moving instinctively to the pistol inside his leather coat. As he slowly relaxed, he noticed Charlie watching him. His steely gaze fastened on the boy - a chilling, ice-blue stare that was the last thing many men had seen. Then he suddenly crossed his eyes. Charlie gave a muffled snort of laughter.

No. They were not lonely when they were together. They were the Clan.

Jack Thane entered his chambers and drew back the veils surrounding the main room. Golden light was wafting through an open window, and a soft breeze carried the smell of ripe apples across his living space. Thane frowned.

On a chair in the centre of the chamber sat Math, sheathed in black velvet, hands clasped demurely on her lap.

"I don't remember inviting you to my rooms, Mistress Math," the wizard said curtly.

Math walked to the window, where dying sunlight framed her white hair and turned it rich copper.

"Being one of the Lords bores you, Jack Thane," she said. "Does it not?"

The sorcerer was taken aback, then gave the question proper consideration.

"I could think of more enjoyable ways to pass the centuries," he admitted.

"I agree." Math absently batted an insect that dared venture too near her face. "But we cannot be out there dancing and singing with the rest of the Galhadrians and ruling them too."

"I would say they require very little ruling," Thane said blackly, sinking onto the eiderdown bed. "They don't exactly do a lot."

"Yes. I preferred Galhadria before the civil war, myself. Back then, our people were more adventurous. More… passionate."

"And the most adventurous and passionate were the ones who rebelled and were destroyed. What you say is close to treason."

Math laughed dismissively.

"You were very quick to spot that the Dolorous Stroke had occurred," she continued, suddenly changing the subject.

The Dolorous Stroke. Thane frowned again at its very mention. It was an ancient spell designed to prevent another uprising. It stated that, should two magical forces go to war, the first side to kill one of the enemy would be destined to lose. And it had been struck against *their* enemy, the Gorrodin Rath. Which meant they were doomed.

"If you have a point, get to it," Thane said.

"You were also quick to act on that discovery. You make a good leader in time of crisis, as the other Lords are now aware."

Jack Thane narrowed his eyes.

"What are you insinuating?"

"I notice you are fond of vanishing from time to time, Jack." The use of a sorcerer's first name alone was a breach of etiquette, but Thane was too intrigued to care.

"I revisit my former haunts occasionally, for old time's sake. What of it?"

"Is the land of Toth one of your old haunts? The place where Morgana has gathered the Gorrodin Rath to march on us."

"I have been there." Jack Thane was more guarded now. "I felt someone should keep watch on them, as I always considered the Rath a serious threat. Now I am proved right."

"Indeed you are." Math continued staring out of the window. "You didn't happen to… eh… cross the path of some of their warriors on your trips? Perhaps… kill one."

Jack Thane rose from the bed and drew himself to his full height. His hate-filled look would have turned a lesser adversary into a trembling wreck.

"You accuse me of the Dolorous Stroke!"

"I am only saying out loud what some of my companions are muttering to themselves." Math was undaunted by the wizard's piercing stare.

"Do you think I am some novice, to be goaded by a scattering of troll-men? That I would sacrifice my own people to a war we cannot win?"

"Of course not," Math replied soothingly. She turned from the window, cloak billowing around her. "But if you were responsible for the Dolorous Stroke, Jack Thane, I'm sure you had a good reason. Perhaps to put in motion your *secret* strategy, one you claim will allow us to cheat certain defeat."

Jack Thane regarded her warily.

"I have an idea I am sure will work," he said slowly. "The fact that I keep it to myself does not mean I caused the conflict which must surely come."

"The Dolorous Stroke cannot be overturned by any magic, no matter how strong," Math reminded him. "Possessing the Grail will not change that, for it cannot be used against Morgana. Gorrodin shared its power with her when they were man and wife, remember?"

She narrowed her eyes.

"There is no way for us to win that I can see."

"It is not merely Gorrodin's cup I seek." The wizard tapped his nose. "The boy Peazle has a secret mission only I know. And it will save Galhadria, I promise."

"You are certain?"

"I am."

"You were always too much like Gorrodin, Jack." Math reached out and touched Thane's cheek. "Brilliant and decisive, yet impetuous and arrogant. The mark of a leader, I suppose."

"What are you saying?"

"That I will back you, if this plan is successful. Support you, should you wish to rule."

Her voice suddenly hardened.

"If you fail, however?" She withdrew her hand and slipped it into the folds of her cloak.

"You will die on the Great Wall, defending Galhadria with the rest of us."

# The Journey North

Lilly and Duncan kept their voices low.

"I'm not sure about Uallabh's plan," the girl said quietly. She looked out the window at the formidable rocky screes that made up so much of highland scenery. "As soon as Morgana realizes we've left the rest of the Clan and headed for my father's prison, at the Falls of Eas a Chual Aluinn, she'll send her forces straight back there. They may well beat us to our destination."

"I'm nae scholar, but I see you're referring tae me in the plural."

Lilly took his hand and smiled.

"I thank you for the noble gesture, highlander," she whispered. "There is a password to open Gorrodin's prison, but it only works when used with the Grail. You are human and the cup can change you if you try to weld its power." She tapped her chest proudly. "I intend to go with you and open the cave - I will be there to see my father's suffering ended."

She waved her fingers in front of the highlander's face. Glittering sparks drifted between the tips.

"I may not have much magic but certainly enough to keep up with you, no matter how fast you think you can travel."

Duncan stared out the window while he considered the girl's words.

"I dinnae like it," he said finally. "But I can see that you coming along make senses." He grinned broadly. "Besides, I cannae protect you if you're stuck up in Wick."

"I need no protection," the girl bristled. "Rather, I thought I might look after *you*."

The trees had thinned out as the train topped the Pass of Shin and the purple peaks of a distant mountain range rose slowly over the horizon. Mossy boulders soaked up the light, and sparkling streams crisscrossed the wrinkled olive landscape.

"You are a brave and noble man, Duncan Mac-Phail." Lilly looked at him with admiration. "People like you and Charlie make me proud to have human blood in my veins."

"Let us hope it stays in oor veins and doesnae end up staining the ground."

They noticed the locomotive was gradually slowing down. Finally, the train shuddered to a halt with a tired hiss.

"Is this Lairg? I don't see any station." Shadowjack pressed his face against the glass, trying to look a little further ahead. The pass was behind them now, and the train was sitting motionless in an unbroken sea of heather.

"There's probably another locomotive up ahead, or the points need changed or something." Peazle tried to demonstrate his knowledge of modern transport - though he didn't have a clue what he was talking about.

"There's nae train ahead and nae points." Paul Jessop shook his grey head. "I've travelled back and forward on this line for nigh on 50 years. It's a single track. Only three trains a day, and this is the last. There must be an obstacle blocking the way."

Uallabh was on his feet and standing on the seat in an instant. He opened the little sliding aperture on top of the main window and pushed his head out.

"Careful noo mannie. This train starts up again, and you'll look like Headless Horace o' the Highlands. He was a famous bogle, you know."

The warrior's head shot in again, a tense look on his face.

"Lilly," he said quietly. "You better take a look."

The girl bounced onto her seat and stuck her head out of the aperture on the other side. The woman in the tweed coat lowered her magazine and tutted loudly.

"What do you see?" Charlie asked, sliding into the aisle. By now, the rest of the Clan were on their feet, looking nervously at each other. Peazle climbed onto the rim of the lower window so he could get his head out of the narrow gap above.

"It's just fog."

"Nonsense." It was Paul Jessop again. "This is one of the windiest moors in the highlands. There's not been a fog here the whole time I've travelled this route. And that's nigh on 50 years," he reminded them.

"It's windy, right enough." The pickpocket was holding the bowler hat on with one hand. "But that fog isn't moving an inch. And it's a funny colour. Almost yellow."

Lilly withdrew her head and pulled Peazle roughly back in.

"Stoorhaar!" she gasped.

"Stoor what?"

"A Stoorhaar." The girl slammed the aperture shut and sank into her seat. "It's a mist that dark forces use to travel undetected."

Uallabh looked over at Duncan, anger spreading across his face.

"Why didn't I think of this?" He thumped the back of his seat, releasing a cloud of dust. "Morgana's not waiting for us to arrive anywhere! She's sent some of her forces to attack the train!"

"She wouldn't dare." Lilly shook her head in disbelief. "There are humans on board!"

"What do you think we are? Easter Bunnies?" Charlie was jumping up and down, trying to reach the luggage rack. His fingers scrabbled at the fishing holder containing Excalibur until he managed to dislodge it. Duncan caught the weapon before it hit the ground. He reached up, pulled his own holder from the rack and unsheathed his blade.

There was a strangled sob from further up the train. The woman in the tweed coat was clutching her two frightened children.

"What do you mean, attack the train?" she squeaked. "And why do you have *swords*?"

"How many carriages are behind the engine?" Uallabh was addressing Paul Jessop. The warrior already had a pistol in each hand. The woman gasped and hugged her children tighter.

"Three."

"Put the damned guns away!" Charlie snapped, looking across at the terrified family. The boy was staring at Uallabh, wide-eyed. He didn't seem all that much younger than Charlie.

"Please don't kill us," the woman whispered.

"We're not going to kill you. We're not going to harm you at all." Charlie moved towards her and the woman and children shrank into their seats. "We're on your side, madam. But there's something outside the train that means us all harm."

The woman tried to hide the whimpering kids in the folds of her voluminous coat. Duncan now held his sword in one hand and Excalibur in the other.

"Mrs McCusker." Paul Jessop obviously knew the petrified family. He got up shakily and pointed to the window behind her. "Out there."

Yellow-green banks of fog were drifting past the train, so thick they seemed to be scraping along the glass.

"These queer-looking folk are telling the truth." the old man said with utter conviction. He turned to Lilly.

"The Stoorhaar is an old legend in these parts, spun to scare wee bairns, but I know it is real. I came across one, once before - a long time ago - and barely escaped with my life."

"You're all insane." Mrs McCusker's eyes were as wide as saucers, and she looked like she was on the verge of a mental breakdown herself.

The sliding door at the front of the carriage opened suddenly. Uallabh and Duncan whirled, weapons pointing. Mrs McCusker squealed.

The train driver stumbled into the carriage and sank to his knees.

"Monster," he croaked. "There's a monster in the fog."

# The Stoorhaar

"Shadowjack, get the rest of the train's passengers into this carriage," Uallabh barked. "Do it now."

"Try not to panic them," Charlie added.

Shadowjack snatched the driver's hat from the man's bowed head and stuck it on his own curly thatch. He raced through the sliding doors at the other end of the carriage and vanished into the compartment beyond.

"Fire! Fire at the back of the train!" They heard him bellowing. "Everybody forward before you're burned to a crisp! Prawn Cocktail flavour, most likely!"

Charlie winced.

"You saw a Stoorhaar before?" Lilly turned to Paul Jessop.

"What's a stoohaa mummy?" the little girl asked pleadingly.

"It's just an old highland story, sweetie. Told by superstitious crofters and the like." The woman patted her daughter's head protectively and shot the old man a filthy look. "It's not real."

The girl looked across at Paul Jessop for confirmation, but he could give her none.

"I ran into one on Ben Armine in 1969." Jessop bit his lip at the memory. "Something in the fog took a sheep right in front of my eyes."

"You're lucky to be alive," Lilly said.

"If I didn't take my shotgun everywhere, I wouldn't be. Took both barrels to scare whatever it was away."

Mrs McCusker gave a groan of dismay at everyone's behaviour.

"You carry a shotgun all the time?" Uallabh asked.

"Of course. I'm a gamekeeper."

"Then get it!"

The sliding doors opened and a stream of people poured into the carriage, though they stopped in alarm when they saw the occupants. Uallabh and Duncan were standing in the middle of the corridor, bristling with weapons. Paul Jessop was perched precariously on the back of a seat, pulling a huge shotgun down from the luggage rack.

"What the hell is going on?" A large, heavy-set man with a bushy beard, fisherman's cap and weatherproof jacket threw his arms wide, stopping the rest of the bewildered passengers from coming any further into the compartment.

"Come on in, Ben Harper," Paul Jessop said, lowering his gun. He seemed to know everyone on the train. "The engine appears to be under attack."

"Attack ye say. By these jokers?" The big man glared suspiciously at the Clan.

"No, no. These folks are eh.... circus performers," the old man replied quickly, showing his mind was agile, even if his body wasn't. "The tall one's Honest John Plain the Wild West Sharpshooter. And that one with the long hair throws swords."

The Clan looked at him with astonishment. Uallabh recovered first, whirling both guns expertly around his fingers.

"Howdy," he said laconically. Charlie did a perfect back flip in his seat.

"I'm an acrobat." He gave a low bow. Five or six juggling balls suddenly appeared in Lilly's hand, spinning through her blurred fingers, before disappearing again. Mrs McCusker's daughter giggled.

"And the big eejit who's running around shouting fire?"

"Circus strongman," Charlie said without hesitation.

"We asked him to get everyone in here." Paul Jessop was unable to keep a roguish smile off his face. "We appear to be in a wee bit of trouble."

Ben Harper motioned and the rest of the passengers began to edge into the carriage. There were another two men, a youth and a woman with a young boy.

"Aye. So you say." Harper stood with his hands on his hips. "What's aw this nonsense about an attack on the train?"

"There's a Stoorhaar outside." Paul Jessop looked unperturbed.

"Och, come on now, Mr Jessop." Ben Harper gave the man an incredulous look. "That's an old wife's tale. I'm surprised at…"

Mrs McCusker let loose a piercing scream, cutting the fisherman off. She was backing away from the window, shaking her head in disbelief.

The yellow mist had obscured the scenery outside, and total silence enveloped the train. They could hear no birds, no wind; even the noise of the idling train engine was gone.

"I saw something in the fog!" Mrs McCusker was pointing in horror. Her children had disappeared under the nearest seats.

A head appeared at the window.

It was a glistening grey, with dead fish eyes and pouting, tooth-ridged lips. But its sheer size was what horrified the occupants – the scaly cranium must have been four feet across. The head flicked quickly to the side, slick, papery skin squealing across the glass like a wet finger. A long body, resembling that of a giant eel, flashed past the windows, travelling the length of the carriage in seconds. Then the creature was gone into the pea-souper.

"Ye Gods. It's a sea serpent," Ben Harper hissed.

"On top of a mountain?" the smaller man behind him spluttered. He was wearing identical gear to Harper. In fact, all the men behind were dressed like him - Charlie guessed he was the captain of a fishing boat and the others were members of his crew. Either that, or everyone in the highlands shared the bigger man's fashion sense.

"It's a Stoorworm." Lilly was bouncing from seat to seat, slamming the upper windows shut. "They swim through the fog. Usually in pairs. And the mist itself is poisonous."

Shadowjack Henry appeared at the back of the little group.

"Shut every window and door on the train," Uallabh shouted to him. "Block up any vents. Do it now!"

The blacksmith nodded and vanished again.

Ben Harper turned to his crew. "Karston, Davie, Sean. Go with the strongman. Give him a hand, then get right back here."

The two men and the youth turned and hurried back the way they had come.

"You, missus. Take your wee kiddie and put him under a seat." Ben Harper was obviously used to giving orders, and the second woman complied immediately. The captain strode over to Paul Jessop.

"I mind you telling me about thon Stoorworm in a pub in Thurso. I thought you were having me on."

"1969. I'll never forget it. I was on a hill in…"

"I apologise for no believing you, but mebbie now isnae the time for a wee story." Harper rounded on Lilly instead. "And how does a lassie like you know so much about yon beastie?"

"I'm a Gypsy," the old lie rolled easily off Lilly's tongue. "We have legends about the Stoorworm just as you do in the highlands."

There was a crash against the side of the train and the worm's head squashed disgustingly against the glass. Its skin flattened out on the window like a lump of ancient dough, then it was gone again, leaving a wide sweaty smear.

"That's no legend!"

"Can it tip the train?" Mrs McCusker whimpered.

"It's a big creature, right enough, but this train weighs about forty tons," the driver piped up between coughs. His face was grey and his breathing laboured. "The lassie's right about the poison, though."

He hauled himself unsteadily to his feet.

"I stopped the train when I saw the fog and tried to close the cab window as it started seeping in, but I caught one mouthful and was almost out cold. The cab's full of the stuff. I can't get back in to move the engine again."

The head crashed into the window. This time, there was a chorus of screams and shouts. The children under the seats began to cry.

The fishermen and Shadowjack piled back into the front carriage.

"We've sealed up every crack, boss," one crew member barked, wiping perspiration from his brow. It was cold in the carriage and Charlie guessed the sweat was made more by fear than exertion.

Mrs McCusker was huddled between seats, holding a mobile phone to her ear.

"You have to help us, officer," she sobbed. "We're on the Wick train, being attacked by giant worms in a poisonous fog. No, it's not a practical joke!"

"Don't be daft, woman!" Ben Harper snapped. "The Lairg Police aren't going to believe that. Tell them it's a chemical gas leak or something."

It was too late. The head smashed against the train again and the window exploded.


Inspector Archer sat in the canteen at St Leonard's police station in Edinburgh, watching his plate of greasy egg and chips go cold. Occasionally the uniforms in the room gave him a curious glance, but he didn't seem particularly friendly, so they left him alone. Most of them didn't even know Archer was a fellow officer. At the table next to him, a group of young recruits were talking about their strangest cases to date.

"So I got to the graveyard and half the headstones had been pushed over," one constable was saying.

"Ach, that's just vandals."

"No. It was worse than that. The whole graveyard was… dug up. I mean every inch. There were bones and everything on the surface. A tree had been completely uprooted. And there were worms everywhere. Millions of them. It was totally raj."

"All right. So it was… a lot of vandals."

"Aye. Well, a woman in one of the tenements did give a statement. Said she saw a bunch of kids and a couple of adults running away from the scene. Said one of the kids was wearing a bowler hat, of all things."

Inspector Archer's head shot up.

"Talking of worms…" a policewoman spooned a forkful of watery pasta into her mouth. "We just got the strangest report over the radio. Some hysterical woman called the police at Lairg a few minutes ago."

"Where's Lairg?"

"It's away up north, but the police there radioed us to ask if we had any reports of a chemical spill in the highlands." The policewoman waved her fork at the other officers. "She claimed the Wick train was being attacked by a poisonous fog filled with flying worms or something."

"Where's Wick?"

"Jeez? Did you not study geography at school?"

Inspector Archer pushed away his plate and stood.

"Excuse me," he said, as politely as he could manage, though excitement coursed through every inch of his lanky frame. "Could you tell me where I can find your commanding officer? I need to ask him a big favour."

Fifteen minutes later, he was speeding north in an unmarked police car.

# The Baggage Car

The Stoorworm forced its bloated, shimmering body through the shattered train window, blank grey eyes searching calmly for its nearest victim. Uallabh and Duncan threw themselves sideways, an instant before razor-sharp teeth snapped shut in the place they had been standing. Paul Jessop and Peazle sank silently onto the floor and Charlie and Lilly flipped over their seat backs, as the monster swerved, buried its jaws in the musty upholstery and ripped out a torso sized chunk.

Shadowjack and the passengers from the other compartment were at the far end of the carriage, beckoning frantically to the kids under the seats. The Stoorworm veered back towards Duncan, but the highlander grasped the luggage rail and swung himself adroitly into the netting, as the gaping mouth sailed past. Mrs McCusker was screaming at the top of her lungs, trapped in her seat by the creature's slimy body, just behind what appeared to be gills. The Stoorworm tried to twist back round to get at her, but its bulk made it impossible to manoeuvre between the train seats, and the petrified woman's very proximity kept her just out of reach of its slashing teeth. Her children were sheltering in the iron framework under the seats, wailing hysterically.

The creature gave an ear-piercing shriek and began to inch its body out of the window to free itself for another attack. Great wads of flesh rolled into ridges behind the head as it fought to pull itself back from the confines of the broken aperture.

"Don't let the beast out!" Lilly shouted, flat on her back between two seats. "Its body is all that's stopping the fog getting in."

Duncan rolled out of the luggage rack and landed on the upholstery below. Using it as a trampoline, he bent his knees and flew into the air, sword held in front of him. He collided with the creature and his blade buried itself in the translucent flesh right behind the bony ridged head. The monster gave another screech and wrenched itself backwards, but the sword caught on the window fame, temporarily stopping its exit. Uallabh stepped forward and emptied both guns into the straining Goliath's flank. The creature hardly seemed to feel it. Charlie sprang up from where he had been hiding.

"Duncan. Excalibur! To me."

Duncan leapt nimbly back from the grinding jaws and tossed the second sword sideways. The boy caught it and launched himself over the top of the Stoorworm's body. Sliding headfirst down the other side, he plunged the sword into the monster and let go, landing upside down on Mrs McCusker's lap. She grabbed him in a maniacal bear hug and held on, howling uncontrollably.

The Stoorworm bucked in agony. Excalibur was no ordinary weapon and, though the monster was too big to kill with one thrust, the Great Sword was causing it extreme distress. It tried to reverse again, but both protruding blades caught against the buckled window frame and stopped the creature getting out. It gave up trying to free itself and fixed its saucer-shaped eyes on Uallabh, who was backing quietly away. The warrior turned to run and tripped over one of Mrs McCusker's children, crawling silently to safety along the aisle floor.

The creature reared up over the prone humans, its mouth widening to an impossible size. Uallabh's mouth opened too, in a doomed plea. The child below him covered its eyes.

There was a deafening roar, then another, and the Stoorworm's head exploded. Gouts of green blood and lumps of grey flesh fountained across the carriage, showering the passengers.

Paul Jessop lowered his shotgun, acrid smoke floating from both barrels.

"It worked in 1969 too." He gave a wry smile.

Peazle rose up from between two gore-splattered seats. A shard of window glass jutted from the side of his temple and blood was running down his nose and congealing under one eye. His face and clothes were covered in green goo, and a large lump of oily flesh protruded from the top of his waistcoat.

"That was truly unpleasant," he said weakly.

"Fetch your swords and get ready to run." Lilly was down on her knees, peering under the seat. "Come, children," she said. "The Stoorworm is dead."

"I'm scared," a little voice came from the darkness.

"But we have to move," the girl gently urged. "When we pull the swords out of the Stoorworm, it'll will fall back through the window, and poison gas will flood in."

She hesitated, then decided that the truth was the best option.

"Plus, there's another one out there, and it's not going to take kindly to us killing its kin."

There was silence under the seats. Charlie prised himself loose from Mrs McCusker's vice-like grip and slid onto the floor, squeezing under the flaccid, bloody chin of the dead Stoorworm.

"My name is Charlie Wilson," he said to the wide eyes under the seat. "I'm hardly any older than you, and I'm really scared too. But the only way to get out of this is to be brave and pull together. Remember, you have your mothers to protect, don't you?"

After a long pause, the children emerged cautiously from the darkness, tracks of their tears streaking dirty cheeks. Mrs McCusker gave her offspring a timid smile and a little wave to indicate she was OK. She eased out of her seat and skirted the dead leviathan, never taking her eyes off it, as if she expected the creature to spring to life at any moment. Once she was clear, the children grasped her hands and led her towards the safety of the next compartment. The rest of the passengers followed them.

Duncan grasped his sword hilt and put one foot against the slippery side of the Stoorworm.

"Ready, Charlie?"

The boy grasped Excalibur and signalled to the highlander that he was. He and Duncan pulled the swords out simultaneously. The creature's own dead weight pulled it back through the window, and a yellow torrent of fog cascaded into the empty gap, like water flooding a breeched ship. Charlie and Duncan retreated, holding their breath, sprinting into the second carriage and shutting the door.

"What do we do now?" asked one of the crewmen.

"Same again, I suppose," Ben Harper said. "If we're lucky, these circus folk can kill the second one the same way they did the first. Then we shut ourselves in the baggage compartment and wait for help to arrive."

"I don't think…" the driver began, but Mrs McCusker was thumping him on the shoulder, fist crammed against her mouth. She pointed behind the uniformed man with a fluttering hand.

A second eel-like head, as big as the first, was watching them from the murk outside the window. Paul Jessop swung his gun again.

"No, wait!" Uallabh held up a hand. "Fire through the glass and the fog will get in."

"Dinnae worry, son. All my ammunition is in the carriage we just left."

"Damn. Mine too," the warrior admitted shamefacedly.

"This one's doing something different," Duncan said, cautiously lowering his sword.

The worm floated in the mist, regarding them with what seemed like cold indifference. Every few seconds, it inched forward, so it almost touched the window, then jerked back with a rippling motion. The children disappeared under a new set of chairs.

"It wants us to fire. Pretending to attack but ready to dodge away."

The passengers moved back and forth, mirroring the monster's subtle motions, ready to flee at any second.

"It's smart! It's trying to figure out a better way to get at us."

The Stoorworm slid slowly to the side and drifted off into the fog. Mrs McCusker heaved a sigh of relief.

"I don't like this one wee bit." Uallabh was twisting and turning, trying to look through every window at once.

"Maybe it's seen a nice juicy bus."

There was a quiet whoosh and the Stoorworm's tail slammed against the window nearest Mrs McCusker. The poor woman almost fainted on her feet. A thick blue crack appeared the length of the window, splitting the vanishing tail into a deadly double prism.

"Everybody into the last carriage!" roared Shadowjack, pulling squealing children from under seats and dragging them with him. "That window won't stand another blow!"

The passengers made a mad dash for the connecting door, pushing and shoving each other into the baggage compartment. As they ran, the Stoorworm's tail crashed into the damaged window again, breaking it into a thousand pieces. Uallabh, still in the doomed carriage, threw himself to the floor as shards of flying glass filled the top half of the car and embedded themselves in the opposite wall. He rolled over and emptied the last few rounds from his pistols at the ruined window. But the tail was gone, and yellow-green mist was already pouring through the hole. The warrior staggered to his feet and flung himself into the baggage compartment. Shadowjack slammed the door behind him.

"We're being outsmarted by a flying fog fish," the blacksmith said grumpily.

The baggage compartment was full of crates and boxes, lit only by overhead lights. To everyone's relief, there were no big windows in this carriage – only small, elongated portals of thick smoked glass near the top. Because it carried goods rather than people, the baggage car was designed with security in mind rather than giving a good view. The passengers sank grate-fully to the floor, breathing heavily.

"Try the mobile phones again. See if we can get help," Ben Harper ordered.

"We've been trying, captain. The signal can't pen-etrate this fog."

"I got through once, but I don't think they believed me." Mrs McCusker gave a sorrowful sniff.

"When the train doesn't turn up at Lairg, they'll send someone. Eventually."

"I think we have to make a move before that," Lilly was looking around. "There's a definite greenish tinge to the air in here."

"The baggage car is built differently from the rest of the train." The driver still looked sick and pale, but he was finally able to talk normally. "Hasnae got any real windows, but it's not airtight like a normal car-riage." He gave a racking cough. "No passengers, see, so it doesnae matter if it's draughty. Lots of little holes everywhere."

"Let's start finding those and plugging them up."

"That's impossible," the driver began to object. "There's no way…"

He caught sight of the cowering children and quickly shut up.

"C'mon now, kids," Shadowjack tore the lid off the nearest crate without the slightest effort. "You look for any wee gaps in the walls. Then we'll see if there's something in these boxes we can use to cover them - blankets and the like. Up and at 'em."

Terrified though the children were, they sprang to attention - Shadowjack Henry was almost as frightening as the Stoorworm. Charlie helped them rummage through the numerous boxes, while Mrs McCusker, Peazle, Duncan and the crewmen felt around the walls for cracks. Paul Jessop sat on the largest crate and directed operations. Eventually, the other woman joined in.

"I'm Mrs Mcnab," she said, offering her hand to Mrs McCusker. "Met you a couple of times in the Co-op in Thurso."

The driver crawled over to Uallabh and Ben Harper.

"This isnae going to work," he whispered. "The baggage compartment's got more holes than a sieve. Our only chance is to try and drive the train out of the fog. I left the engine running. All we have to do is release the brake and push the throttle."

"Only we can't get to the cab without suffocating or getting eaten," Uallabh pointed out listlessly. Since his double brush with death, the fight seemed to have been knocked out of him.

"I can run through the carriages holding my breath." Ben Harper got to his feet. "What do the brake and throttle look like?"

"Two levers on the control panel. Green and red. Push them both forward."

"Don't be daft," Duncan had overheard the conversation. "You'd never make it that far."

"I'm a captain." Ben Harper gave a nervous smile. "I'm supposed tae go down with my ship. Well… train."

"No." Charlie joined in. "These things are after us, not you. It's all our fault. One of us will have to go."

"Oh, thanks, boy," Uallabh said caustically. By now, the rest of the passengers were listening intently.

"Why is it your fault? What do you mean?" Mrs McCusker was still desperately seeking an explanation of the surrounding madness.

"Now's not really the time to go into it." Charlie indicated the faint layer of yellow slowly spreading across the floor. "But our… eh… circus is fighting some very dark forces. We didn't mean you to get caught in the middle."

"What in the name of Harry's knitting are these?" Shadowjack was still foraging in the crates. He hauled a double tank, topped with a gauge, out of the straw packing. A mask on the end of a short tube dangled from the cylinders.

One of the crewmen came over and inspected the equipment.

"Scuba gear," he said. "Must be on route tae Wick. Divers use them for minor repairs on oil rigs."

Shadowjack just stared.

"I didn't understand any of that."

"You use them to breathe underwater, big man." Ben Harper gave a broad smile. "Or, if you're desperate enough, in a poisonous fog."

# The Fight at the Pass of Shin

While Ben Harper checked the diving equipment for faults, an unspoken question hung in the air, as unpalatable as the fog outside.

"Who's going to go?" Peazle said finally.

"I will." Duncan, as usual, showed no hesitation.

"No. I'll go," Shadowjack butted in. "These tanks are heavy. I can carry them faster than the rest of you."

"Neither of you know anything about modern technology." Charlie looked up from the crate he was rummaging in.

"I can push a couple of levers well enough. And I certainly know how to breathe."

"It's not as easy as that," Ben Harper broke in. "I should do it. I've had experience with Scuba gear."

"So has Uallabh, I'll bet," Peazle said, but the warrior simply scowled and shook his head.

"It has to be someone small." Lilly's voice cut through the argument. Charlie and Peazle looked at her in alarm and the other children scampered behind one of the crates.

"The carriages are full of thick fog," the girl continued. "Try to go fast, and you'll be crashing into seats and debris that you can't see until the Stoorworm cuts you down. But someone small can crawl along the aisle, between the seats, even with the tanks strapped on. It's the only way anyone will reach the cab."

She looked around at the others.

"I'm the smallest," she added unnecessarily. "It has to be me."

"Naw. That's suicide, lassie," Ben Harper objected.

"Eh. I can... actually... ehm... make myself invisible." Lilly said tentatively. "Only for a little while, but I have that much power, at least."

Her voice petered out as she realised that the whole box car was staring at her.

"Invisible, is it?" Paul Jessop raised a white flecked eyebrow. Ben Harper took off his hat and scratched his head.

"You're a wee bit more than a circus performer, aren't you?"

"A wee bit."

"That's why you can't go." Peazle put an end to the awkward discussion. "What happens if you do come across the Stoorworm? Magical creatures can't fight each other remember?" He tapped his thin chest. "I'm as small as you. Can you make *me* invisible?"

Lilly nodded.

"Then it's settled." The boy pulled his bowler hat tightly onto his head. "As a pickpocket, I'm already an expert at not drawing attention to myself."

"Nice try." As Charlie spoke, a fresh rivulet of blood escaped from under the rim of Peazle's hat and trickled down his forehead. "But you can't see properly, even without any fog."

The boy was still pulling items from crates and studying them, stuffing some into pockets and discarding others. He straightened up, compared a fish knife he held in one hand to a grappling hook in the other, then gave both a tentative swing.

"I'm small. I've done scuba diving on holiday with my parents. Strap the tanks on me." The boy turned and spread his arms wide, weapon in each hand. "Go on, before I change my mind."

"The mist in here is getting thicker," Mrs McCusker said, furiously stuffing paper towels into a drill hole in the floor. "Whoever is going better do it fast."

"I don't like this." Ben Harper picked up the tanks with a grunt and began to fasten them to Charlie's back. "Sending a wee boy."

"Really? I'm just loving it," Charlie replied acidly, his knees almost buckling under the weight of the tanks. He stood erect, not without some difficulty, and took a deep breath.

"Take Excalibur."

"He can't. The stupid thing is made of Faerie silver and isn't affected by my weak magic." Lilly said irreverently. "I can't make it invisible."

"Hell. I've got half a dozen weapons." Charlie was wedging the fish knife in his belt and looking for somewhere to fasten the grappling hook. "I could start a war with what's in those crates."

"A wee blade's not going to make much of an impression on that big beast," Peazle said doubtfully.

"What do you want him to do? Charm his way past it?"

"Stop it, all of you." Lilly raised her arms, took a deep breath, and then thrust both hands forwards, fingers spread.

"Get ready, Charlie," she said. "Take care."

The boy vanished. There was a gasp from the crewmen and the children. The mothers stopped blocking up holes and stared in amazement.

"I'd be the world's best gamekeeper if I could do that," Paul Jessop whistled. "Aye, and poach on the side too."

"Am I invisible?" The boy's trembling voice came from nowhere.

"Either that, or we've all gone blind," Duncan replied in an awed tone. "Shadowjack, hammer on the back of the carriage, distract that big worm thingie. Give Charlie a chance tae get oot the other way."

Shadowjack motioned the children and together, they began to yell and bang on the back of the baggage car.

There was a clank, a grunt and the sound of hollow breathing, like someone sucking noisily through a tube. The carriage door suddenly slid open and shut again. Then the sound was gone and so was Charlie.

As soon as he was through the sliding doors, the boy dropped to his knees and began to crawl. The fog in the carriage was so thick and murky it was like moving along the bottom of some polluted sea - Charlie couldn't even see his hands in front of him. Then he realised he couldn't see his hands anyway and chuckled, despite himself.

Inch by inch, he felt his way, the scuba tanks already causing his arm muscles to ache and his lungs to strain. Shards of glass littered the carriage floor and stuck in his palms, until the boy bit his lip in pain. By the time he was halfway down the carriage he was leaving little smears of blood on the dirty floor, and his breath was coming in ragged gasps. Every few feet, the air tanks caught on the seats flanking him and he had to reverse and free them before carrying on. The silence was as thick as the fog, making his laboured breathing thunder in his ears.

There was no sign of the Stoorworm.

A shin-high yellow film now covered the floor of the baggage car, forcing the occupants to stand. The children were huddled together on top of one of the crates. Mrs McCusker and Mrs Mcnab had wrapped scarves round their mouths but were still bravely stopping up holes in the carriage wall with rags and paper.

"I shouldn't have let that wee laddie go." Ben Harper had his ear to the carriage door, listening for any sound of Charlie. "He's helluva brave, though."

"He most certainly is." Peazle sat miserably on a box, rag pressed against his bloody forehead. "Used scuba gear on holiday? His parents haven't two pennies to rub together. I bet he's never even been in a boat."

Charlie's head bumped into something solid. He reached out on either side, as far as he could, but there was no way past the barrier. For a second he felt a rising panic, thinking he had taken some kind of wrong turn. Then he realised he had crawled the length of the second carriage and reached the door on the opposite side. He gave a silent prayer, for his back was now aching, and his arms felt as if they might not support him much longer. With his body flat against the wood panel, he felt around above him until one lacerated hand grasped the handle. He cautiously slid the door open, scuttled through and began crawling again.

The fog had now reached the thighs of those in the baggage compartment. Duncan paced back and forth, scowling, still holding a sword in each hand. He hated being powerless to act, especially while Charlie was out there, risking his life.

"Best stay still, lad," said Sean, one of Harper's crewmen. "You're using up mair oxygen, doin that."

With a muttered curse, Duncan went and sat on a crate, where he had to make do with tapping his foot impatiently.

"I don't understand," Shadowjack said suddenly. "That fog outside is so thick you can't see an inch."

"I know. But all Charlie has to do is follow the aisle and he'll get there."

"I'm not talking about Charlie." The big man got off his crate and looked up at the little misted windows above. "How do Stoorworms see in it?"

Lilly clasped a hand to her mouth.

Realisation slowly spread over Ben Harper's face.

"They must be like sharks – hunting using smell as well as vision." He tapped his thick, bulbous nose.

"They don't have to see prey. They smell them."


Charlie was halfway through the front carriage, wheezing like a pair of bellows, when the Stoorworm struck. The boy felt a blast of hot air across his neck and the fog around him darkened under a huge shadow. Then something slammed into his back with a force that crushed him to the ground, almost knocking the scuba mask from his face. His chest whacked against the carriage floor and his lungs emptied of air. The round back of the grappling hook bounced off a rib with so much force it almost broke. Fighting to suck oxygen into his empty lungs, Charlie could hear the creature's teeth grinding across the surface of the scuba tanks, as it tried to gain purchase on his exposed flesh. Snapping jaws slipped off the metal cylinder, and the worm pulled back with an enraged shriek.

Charlie scuttled forward but only gained a few feet before the creature attacked again. The boy twisted his head in time to see the Stoorworm filling the broken window and lunging towards him. Its slavering maw clamped onto the scuba tanks again and, this time, the monster held on.

The Stoorworm reared up, pulling Charlie off his hands and knees and into the air, like some fish caught on a hook. With its prey firmly locked in its jaws, the monster reversed out of the window, dragging the boy with it. Charlie clawed at his invisible waistband, trying to reach the fish knife, but the straps of the scuba gear had been pulled so tightly against his chest he couldn't get it free.

There was a deafening bang and Charlie shuddered violently in the air. The Stoorworm's teeth had ruptured one of the tanks! A jet of compressed oxygen shot into the creature's mouth, and it swung sideways with a choked cry. Charlie spun into the air, hit the opposite wall and landed on his back in one of the seats. The tanks smashed into his spine for a second time, sending a searing jolt of agony through his body. A surge of nausea rose in his throat and the boy's head swam. Oxygen hissed out of the tank and enveloped him in a pure cloud, clearing the fog away and giving him a proper view of his attacker for the first time.

The Stoorworm was thrashing its head from side to side, near the roof of the carriage, exhaling the poisonous oxygen from its gaping jaws in mighty puffs. It dipped its slobbering head towards the helpless boy and prepared for a final assault.

Charlie put his hand inside his jacket and pulled out another object he had found in the baggage car crate. When it was visible, it was a small red cylinder with a warning label on the side – a ship's emergency flare.

"I'd say this was an emergency," the boy growled through gritted teeth.

He pulled the trigger.

A plume of red poured from the barrel and shot into the Stoorworm's snarling mouth. The creature reared upwards in anguish, its head almost demolishing the roof. Billowing crimson smoke and flames erupted from the mighty jaws as the flare exploded inside its throat.

For a moment, Charlie knew exactly what a dragon looked like.

Then the pale malevolent eyes glazed over, and the Stoorworm slid lifelessly out of the window.

The boy rolled off the seat and stumbled along the aisle, a jet of oxygen forcing enough of the fog aside to let him see the carriage door ahead. But the tank itself was almost empty and the boy's head was aching. He burst into the locomotive cab, felt for the levers on the control panel and pushed them. There was a throaty roar from the engine and the train lurched forwards. Charlie lost his balance, stumbled and fell - then blackness closed over him.

He awoke, lying stretched out on one of the seats. Outside he could see the tops of trees floating past and a welcome wind blew in through the shattered window. Around him, a ring of concerned faces peered down.

"We owe you our lives, laddie," Ben Harper said, ruffling the boy's hair. His crewmen nodded in agreement. Paul Jessop winked at him. Mrs McCusker and Mrs Mcnab looked like they were ready to swoon with gratefulness and their children regarded him with something akin to hero-worship. Behind them, he could see the Clan waving.

Only Uallabh held back, an odd expression of distaste on his face. Lilly pushed her way through to Charlie's side, leaned over and gave him a kiss on the lips.

"You are a real hero," she whispered.

The cab door slid open and the train driver's beaming face appeared round the frame.

"We've left all trace of thon fog behind," he announced happily. "The train will be arriving at Lairg station in a few minutes. Late as usual."

"You have our deepest gratitude, son." Ben Harper fingered the cap in his hand. "There are things going on with this strange band of yours that we cannae pretend tae understand. But, if we can do anything to help, we surely will."

He looked around.

"That means all of us."

The crewmen, women and kids nodded in agreement.

Charlie studied the ring of faces and a wild idea began to form in his mind. Ben Harper was big and had a beard. Sean was tall. Mrs McCusker and Mrs Mcnab had three children between them. And now that the youngest of Harper's crew had removed his cap, Charlie saw that he had long black hair, like Duncan.

The boy sat up, wincing at the pain in his back.

"You want to help?" he said brightly. "As a matter of fact, I know exactly how you can."

# Part 2

*To him the long years and ages have been but as days. He lies in magic sleep. But the day will come when the strong enchantment that bound him will be broken, and he will come forth to behold the changes that have been wrought by more potent arts than his, and all the wonders of this later time.*

Charles Henry Hanson. *Stories of the Days of King Arthur*

# Lairg

Inspector Archer was parked by the side of the road, mobile phone pressed to his ear, in a vain attempt to combat the devastating effect the surrounding mountains were having on reception.

"Is this Lairg station?" he yelled. "I'm trying to get some information about the Wick train… Wick!… No. I'm with Birmingham CID… Yes, that's in England, I know. But I'm not there, I'm…"

Inspector Archer squinted through his windshield. Rich pastureland swept upward, fading into jagged peaks on either side of the single track road, as far as he could see. The tops of the mountains were drifting in and out of a rainy mist.

"I'm in the highlands somewhere… Look, I need to know if the Wick train has arrived in Lairg yet… Ah… right. Two hours late."

The Inspector held the phone away from his head as the station master launched into a shouted tirade about the disruption to the schedule, making him miss his tea.

"Was there anything odd about the train?" Archer interrupted. "Broken windows, you say? Dents in the roof."

He grabbed his notebook and flipped it open. The station-master had begun another heated monologue about how he had to clean up broken glass, that the carriages had been covered in muck that smelled of fish and how the train wasn't fit to continue its journey, so the passengers were going to have to wait till morning for the next one.

Inspector Archer took a deep breath.

"I'm looking for… certain individuals that might be among the passengers." He looked at the description of the graveyard party, scribbled down by the Edinburgh police.

"I haven't got many details, but there are a couple of men. One is big with a beard. There's a girl, two boys and a youth with long hair." He hesitated, then plunged on. "Eh…. one of the children might be wearing a bowler hat. They're there? You're sure?"

The Inspector beeped his horn in triumph and a few startled sheep popped their dirty heads out of the gorse.

"Listen very carefully. I want you to call the local police. Give them my name and ID number and tell them to hold on to these people till I get to Lairg… No, I don't know where I am, but I'm on my way."

Inspector Archer gunned his car to life and spun back onto the road.

Darkness was finally falling. A narrow road skirted the edge of Gruid's wood and, beyond that, the River Shin was turning into a strip of ink. Duncan could no longer see the tree-lined embankment across the water, where the Clan had left the train. The engine driver had stopped briefly, a mile before Lairg, to let them off in the most thickly forested area he knew. They had waded across the river and hidden among the trees until dusk - the driver assured them this area was rarely visited. Then they had tried to snatch some sleep while they waited for night.

Half a dozen yellow streetlights sputtered to life in the distance, marking out Lairg's solitary main road. Duncan slipped back into the trees and began shaking the sleeping bags to rouse each slumbering member of the Clan.

"It's time tae leave," he informed the others, as they crawled reluctantly from the warmth of their sleeping bags. "It's dark enough so nae birds will be flying, or unable to see us if they do."

He offered round a flask of ice-cold water from the river.

"I hope you got some sleep for we'll have tae travel all night, and quickly too. Leave everything that's not essential."

"Like our sanity," Charlie grunted. But Duncan was already heading out of the forest to keep look out on the narrow road that led in the direction of Lairg. The rest of the Clan emerged warily from the trees.

"Wait a minute. Peazle's not here," Shadowjack looked round. "His sleeping bag's empty."

"Och, that's all we need." Duncan snarled. "Does he not realise we have tae make thirty miles on foot this night and get through Lairg without being spotted besides? His wee legs winnae appreciate that, *withoot* any delays."

"Hush. Something's coming." Lilly held up a hand. They heard the sound of an engine, faint but steadily growing louder. The Clan scattered, flattening themselves into the long grass on either side of the tarmac, watching a pair of headlights appeared over the brow of the hill. Monochrome fence posts, trees and scraggly grass bobbed in the double beams, as a tractor and trailer zigzagged erratically down the lane, drew alongside their hiding place and sputtered to a halt.

"I have to say, this is one of the biggest things I've ever stolen." A little light went on in the cab and Peazle's beaming face winked into existence. "Uallabh. Would you consent to take over? I've never really driven before and I can only work the pedals by standing. I can't see properly out the window either."

He hopped down from the cab and the warrior silently took his place. The rest of the Clan climbed into the long, flatbed trailer, filled with bales of straw and covered in tarpaulin. Once they wriggled underneath the plastic covering, they were invisible from the air. If Morgana's spies were on the wing, they would see nothing more suspicious than a tractor man driving through the night to make a dawn delivery.

Uallabh floored the accelerator and the tractor trundled off at a sedate but respectable speed. It rolled down Lairg's silent main street, encountering only one car on the way, then headed into the darkness again. The narrow road kept close to the shore of Loch Shin, though they could no longer see the water. The mountains on the other side of the highway had solidified into a black mass, craggy outlines only visible because they blocked out the stars.

On the tractor rattled, through Dalchork Wood and over Fiag Bridge, past the solitary Overscaig Hotel, its lights blazing at the rim of the dark forest. Fifteen miles further on, near the tip of Loch Shin, a tiny dirt track broke off from the road and headed west. Duncan sat up, tapped on the back of the cab and motioned in that direction. A few minutes later, they reached a scattering of lonely windows, curtains drawn, that marked the hamlet of Corrykinloch. Here the track petered out, so Uallabh parked the tractor in a nearby field and the Clan crept away from the last habitation that marked their journey. The highlander signalled ahead to where two solid chunks of blackness rose on either side of a near-invisible pass.

"Up there? In the dark?" Peazle's jaw dropped in disbelief.

"It's blacker than the Earl of Hell's waistcoat," Shadowjack chimed in.

"You'd rather wait till daylight? Get caught out crossing bare mountains withoot any cover?" Duncan shouldered his pack and fastened his sword to his side.

"Walk steadily and cautiously, and dinnae stray from my footsteps. If I can remember the way, we will reach the Falls by sunrise."

"And if you can't?"

"Then we'll end up dead at the bottom of a cliff." The highlander gave an uncharacteristic bark of laughter and set off into the night, eager to roam once more on the hills he dearly loved.

Inspector Archer pulled to a halt outside Lairg police station, a boxy two-story house with a single police sign on a pole in the garden. The door of the building opened as he walked up the path and a wedge of yellow light spilled over two begonias in plastic pots and a battered welcome mat.

"You made it safely then?" Lairg's only policeman, Constable MacDonald, shook the Inspector's hand and ushered him inside.

"Apart from almost getting run off the road by a tractor and trailer, I'm fine." The Inspector showed the constable his ID and badge, then removed his raincoat.

They were in a study that obviously doubled as the policeman's office. A child's push-along car lay, abandoned, in the middle of the floor, and half a dozen wanted posters were tacked next to a picture of the

Tweenies. With a jolt, Inspector Archer realized that the Tweenies actually looked more sinister.

"What's the story on the train passengers?" he said, quickly turning away.

"Not much." Constable MacDonald opened his notebook and scanned it. "Bunch of fishermen fae Wick. A Mrs McCusker, also from Wick, with her two children. Mrs Mcnab and her son are from just outside Tain. They all appear to be genuine."

The policeman shut his notebook and tossed it to the Inspector.

"And there's an old gamekeeper who wouldn't let go of his shotgun until I threatened to throw him in jail. But I wouldn't say he was the criminal type."

"Nobody called Charlie Wilson?" Archer frowned.

"Not as far as I know."

"Then I need to talk to whichever boy was wearing a bowler hat."

"There's not a lot of space – the holding area is full with that lot - but you can take him upstairs to my living room for some privacy. Tea?"

The constable plugged in an old electric kettle and got some chipped cups emblazoned with *Lairg Folk Festival 1987* from the cupboard.

"Mrs McCusker will have to be present too, seeing how it's her wee boy wi the hat and him being a minor."

The Inspector was standing in the living room, studying a dresser covered in family photographs and darts trophies, when Constable MacDonald ushered Mrs McCusker and her son in. He looked quizzically at Archer.

"I'm inspecting," the Inspector said. Constable MacDonald sighed and closed the door. Archer motioned for the mother and son to sit, and both sank nervously into an old floral sofa, which emitted a flurry of loud boings and almost swallowed them. The pair sat, pale and uncertain, hands trembling on knees which were now higher than their heads. There were a matching set of floral armchairs opposite that looked equally deadly, so the Inspector chose to stand and give himself a height advantage.

Archer had interviewed hundreds of witnesses before, but never with so little material to work on. He didn't even know what he was looking for - except Charlie Wilson, of course. Beside the dresser, a blue budgerigar in a cage puffed up its feathers and chirruped loudly. The boy was still wearing the bowler hat, as well as a bright yellow waistcoat.

"First, just let me just say that you're not in any trouble," the Inspector lied, leaning casually on the mantelpiece, his elbow lost among engraved China bells and miniature Wally Dugs. "I just need the answer to a couple of questions."

The boy nodded, wiping a tired, tear-streaked cheek.

"I need to know what you were doing in Birmingham a couple of days ago, that's all. With a lad called Charlie Wilson."

Mrs McCusker's lips tightened and the boy shook his head vehemently.

"I've never been south of Dundee, mister," he replied unhappily. "I live in Wick with my ma."

He looked at his mother for reassurance.

"Shouldn't we have a lawyer? I don't think we should say anything." The woman was sitting so rigidly she looked like her spine would fracture if anyone coughed.

"You have the right to remain silent…" the budgie whooped. Mrs McCusker glared at it.

"You don't need a lawyer. You're not under arrest." The Inspector addressed the boy again, ignoring Mrs McCusker, skilfully keeping the excitement out of his voice. He knew instinctively that the child was telling the truth - but both mother and son had given a small start at the mention of Charlie Wilson.

"Tell you what, I'll come clean with you if you do the same for me," he continued pleasantly. "What's your name?"

"Cormack."

"Mine is Walter."

The boy smiled.

"Yes. I don't tell many people that. Most call me Inspector." Archer smiled back. Then his mannerisms switched the way only an effective policeman's can.

"Charlie Wilson is in danger, isn't he? And he's only a kid, just like you."

He hammered home the point, even though he hated doing it.

"If something happens to Charlie because I can't find him in time, that will be your fault." He looked evenly at the boy, all trace of friendliness gone.

"Then you *are* in trouble."

Cormack's eyes opened wide and he gave a whimper. He looked at his mother again, pleadingly.

"You say nothing, child." The woman fixed the Inspector with a steely glare. "But the policeman and I want to have a wee talk."

Cormack looked suddenly alarmed.

"Trust me, son," Mrs McCusker said gently. "C'mere."

She removed the bowler hat and kissed his head.

"Away to the loo and wash your face." She looked defiantly at the Inspector, daring him to detain her son further. When Archer gave no response, she gave the child a pat on the behind with the hat and shooed him out of the room.

"Nice young lad," said the Inspector, once Cormack had gone. "You must be proud of him."

Mrs McCusker stayed silent.

"Strange that his clothes don't fit properly," the policeman added.

Mrs McCusker bristled but still said nothing. The Inspector sat on the coffee table across from her so that their heads were nearer the same height.

"I had a peep at the other passengers downstairs," he continued. "Some of their clothes don't fit either. Like they swapped outfits with someone else. As if they were decoys for a group that looked a bit like them."

The woman pointedly avoided his stare.

"I think Charlie Wilson and his... eh... friends were on your train. I think they got off somewhere before Lairg. I think you and the other passengers are covering for them. I just don't know why."

The Inspector leaned farther forwards, forcing himself into Mrs McCusker's line of sight.

"I think you called and reported a monster attacking the train."

Mrs McCusker looked down and the budgie blew a raspberry.

Archer moved closer to the unresponsive woman and whispered in her ear.

"And I think I'm the only policeman in the world who'd believe that phone call wasn't a hoax."

The Inspector picked up the bowler hat from the couch and removed a shard of glittering glass.

"I investigate cases of missing children, Mrs McCusker," he said softly, still inches from her ear. "I *believe* in monsters. For once, I'd like to save a child from one, before it's too late."

Tears glistened in Mrs McCusker's eyes.

"Everything *I* believe in has been sorely tested, Inspector," she said finally. "If Charlie Wilson and his friends are being chased by something evil, and I know they are, I've no proof it's not you."

She struggled to get out of the low slung couch and the Inspector stood and offered his hand.

"As a matter of fact, I think you are genuine," the woman said breathlessly, as Archer pulled her to her feet. "But I promised my son I wouldn't talk, and I don't think any of the rest of the passengers will either. So, if we're not under arrest, my kids and I will be finding a hotel room for the night."

Mrs McCusker turned to see her son smiling at her from the doorway, his face washed and his hair combed.

"Keep the hat." She took Cormack's hand and swept out of the room.

"Fair cop guv," the budgie squeaked.

Archer collapsed wearily into the patterned armchair, bowler on his knees, passing the rim idly through his fingers. He tried it on his head but it was too small. On impulse, he turned it over and looked inside. A tiny bit of paper was sticking out of the crepe lining. With trembling fingers, the Inspector unfolded it.

It was a small section of a touring map showing the area around Lairg. One name had been circled in black pen.

*Eas a Chual Aluinn Falls.*

He got out his mobile and dialled. It was answered at the first ring.

"Mrs Wilson?" he said. "I think I know where your son is going."

# Heading for the Falls

Charlie had almost come to terms with leading a dangerous life. You tried not to think about it until something bad actually happened - then you simply responded. If you responded by not running away, you were considered brave. Charlie didn't think he was particularly brave and his courage was now being sorely tested. Climbing these highland hills, with nothing but cloud riddled moonlight to light the way, brought on a slow creeping dread. The Clan were moving across steep, uneven terrain pocked with hidden holes and warrens that would have been perilous in broad daylight. After a couple of hours, everyone's legs, lungs and hearts were aching, but that was not the worst part. Hostile inclines with summits that vanished into the blackness loomed on every side, creating a world of sinister shadows - and every crack of a twig had Charlie's heart in his mouth. Twice they found themselves feet away from the edge of a near-invisible cliff and retreated in panic.

As he walked, the boy kept repeating one of the last things his father had told him.

*There are two great virtues that a man can have. One is knowing what is right. The other is doing what is right.*

The words comforted and kept him going, even when he longed to give up and lie down, exhausted, in the heather.

He had obviously paid more attention to his father than he realised. And the boy missed his dad all the more for that.

Duncan walked at the head of the Clan throughout the night, worried in a different way. He had only been in this area twice before, both times in daylight - and that was almost two centuries ago. But he had taken time to memorise the lay of the land on Peazle's map - which was a good job, since the pickpocket had left it in Lairg by mistake. And he had a highlander's natural sense of direction and feeling for how the mountains lay.

Unerringly he led them along the side of Creag Riabhach and up and around Loch Nan Sgaraig. They slid on their backsides into the black unknown that finally levelled out at the waters of Gorm Loch Mor, then followed its tributary along the floor of a steep valley that Duncan hoped would come out near the Falls.

He was right. After hours of stumbling through the midnight ravines, they heard a low hiss, rising to a rumble that eventually turned into a roar. Duncan signalled a halt.

"Well. We cannae see the Falls, but there is nae doubt we are close."

Charlie looked at the luminous dial of his watch.

"There's still a couple of hours till dawn," he said. "Maybe we should try and catch a little kip."

"Excellent suggestion." Shadowjack and Peazle already had their sleeping bags out of their rucksacks and were climbing in. Charlie opened his own pack, his frozen fingers fumbling at the strings. With an exhausted groan, he unrolled his sleeping bag, climbed in, and immediately fell asleep.

The boy woke to see a narrow grey light outlining the horizon. He forced his gummy eyes open and looked around. The Clan were strewn around him in an array of red and blue bags, only the tops of their heads visible. The boy propped himself up on one elbow. In front of him, the valley opened out into a flat glen ringed by mountains, though it was still too dark to make out more details of the landscape. Still, there was no mistaking the area. This was once the home of Gorrodin - the same place he had seen after drinking Jack Thane's potion.

Uallabh was sitting on a rock, with his back to the rest of the group, staring at the cold glow of dawn spreading across the east. Charlie wriggled out of the bag and crawled over to him.

The warrior was wearing the long oilskin coat that used to belong to one of the fishermen. Wrapped around him like a cloak, it didn't look much different from his normal attire. Charlie sat on the wide rock next to him.

"You are a brave fighter indeed, lad," Uallabh said, without looking at him.

"So are you."

The warrior remained motionless.

"I have fought to keep alive, that's all."

"No. You could have handed over the cup to us and gone safely on your way. You didn't."

Uallabh began to protest, but Charlie held up his hand.

"You are a brave and noble warrior." The boy hesitated. "You've just lost your nerve."

Startled, Uallabh glanced sideways at him.

"What gave me away?"

"Yesterday on the train. You jumped when a branch hit the window. It was more than just a reflex. You were scared."

"I was." The warrior turned and fixed cold grey eyes on Charlie. "Over the centuries, I have seen all the horrific things that human beings can do to each other. I don't like humanity, and I long ago grew tired of this world. Yet, I have also travelled the globe and seen its natural beauty. I have fought so many times to stay breathing that maybe living is just a habit."

He unfastened the buttons on the weatherproof jacket.

"Whatever the reason, I'm afraid to die, son."

Uallabh brought out a gun from inside the coat and began to check the mechanism with the practised motions of an expert in firearms.

"I was once a fearless fighter. Now I'm just a killer, scared of where his next enemy will strike."

His voice held no trace of pity, either for his victims or for himself.

"Wait here." Charlie got up and ran back to his sleeping bag. He pulled Excalibur from its holder and returned.

The rising sun was beating back shadows across a beautiful heather-covered valley. Beyond that Eas a Chual Aluinn Falls cascaded down the mountainside - half in darkness, half in light - its upper waters sparkling like molten silver.

"You can't be tired of all the people in this world." He indicated behind him, where the Clan were beginning to stir. "Not all of us are bad, are we?"

Once more, an image of Charlie's father sprang into the boy's mind. His dad, who had offered to give up the life he had chosen, to waste away in some bank for the love of his son. The boy had never thought of it that way before.

"If there comes a time when nobody is willing to sacrifice themselves for those they care about," he said. "Then you can truly give up on humanity."

The warrior looked morbidly across the lightening landscape.

"You know as well as I that Morgana won't have left this place completely undefended," he said.

The boy reached out his hand for the gun.

"Why don't I take that?" he asked. "And you take the sword. Like you used to when you were with King Arthur. We'll go and fight together."

Uallabh picked up Excalibur and held it in front of him, watching its blade glint in the crisp radiance of dawn. The warrior slid the gun back into his coat and stepped down off the rock.

"No. If this sword ever belonged to someone other than Arthur, it surely belongs to you." He knelt before Charlie, holding out the weapon, hilt first.

"My Lord," he said, bowing his head.

Surprised, Charlie took the handle. On impulse, he laid the blade gently on Uallabh's shoulder. The warrior clasped both hands together in acknowledgement, then stood and looked out across the valley.

"Let us go to battle."

And he turned and walked into the rising sun.

# Gorrodin

The Clan stared up at the sheer face of the mountain called Leiter Dhuibh. Light inched across the valley floor, pushing the last shadows into mountainous corners as the sun gained height. Half a mile to the left, Eas a Chual Aluinn Falls arced over the top of a sheer incline, then dropped in drifting plumes of white, five hundred feet into a churning river. The air was damp with spray, even at this distance, and the Clan shivered in the shady strip at the base of the cliff. Lilly stood in front of the group, her father's talisman held tightly against her body.

"Where's the cave?" Shadowjack Henry scrutinised the craggy precipice but could see no sign of an entrance.

"Hidden." Lilly's voice was tense, her face a mixture of anxiety and anticipation. "One simple word will open and close it, but not without the key."

She held up the glowing wooden cup.

"This is the key."

"What's the password?" Peazle asked. "It's not Open Sesame, is it?"

"That's two words."

"It is my real name," Lilly said simply. "Nimve."

"Heather. Lilly. Nimve." Peazle smirked. "How many names do you *have*?"

But the others were staring past him. The pickpocket turned and his eyes widened.

The bottom of the cliff was slowly peeling open, bending back on itself like burning paper. The ground began to shake and, with a tooth jarring reverberation, rock parted from solid rock, until a crack the height of a two-story house snaked up the stone face.

A few loose boulders fell and rolled onto the grass, then there was silence. The Clan shuffled around uneasily while Lilly stood immobile, staring intently into the dark fissure.

Gorrodin emerged.

He was tall and thin and wore a dark green cloak over a silver tunic. A battered leather bag hung by his side. His face was pale and drawn, but his eyes were as bright and green as the most precious emeralds.

He saw his daughter and, for the first time in nearly a thousand years, Gorrodin smiled.

Lilly dropped the Grail and ran to him, launching herself into her father's arms, laughing uncontrollably. Gorrodin swept her round, holding her tight, his grateful face pressed against the girl's cheek. Eventually, he put her down and knelt, both hands resting on her shoulders.

"You have remained a child, Nimve," he said softly, stroking her hair.

"I did not want to grow up without you," she replied. Gorrodin clutched her to him again, as if he would never let the girl go.

Charlie felt his own tears welling and Peazle wiped at his eyes with a grubby sleeve. Uallabh and Duncan looked at the ground and Shadowjack coughed and patted his chest, trying to stop emotions getting away with him.

"I'd say our quest was worth this moment alone," he said in a croaky voice.

Gorrodin finally released his child.

"I feel I have slept for an age," he said to her. He had not even looked at the rest of the Clan. "You must show me all, Nimve."

"It's Lilly now, Father."

"Very well, Lilly. Let me see." He placed willowy fingers on either side of the girl's head and stared into her eyes for a long time.

"He's doing his magic thingie," Peazle explained.

At last Gorrodin relaxed, letting both arms fall to his sides.

"Ah," he said sorrowfully. "I see."

He stood up, placing a protective hand on Lilly's arm, and faced the others.

"I can never thank you enough for what you have done. What powers I possess will always work in your favour. You have my word."

He spotted the Grail lying in the grass. Taking his daughter's hand, he walked over and picked it up. But he did not look pleased to see his talisman.

"Morgana will not have left my place of imprisonment unguarded." The wizard looked quickly around. "There was a Thin Place on yonder hill. I sense it is still open, so we must make haste towards it. I have a lifetime of love to shower on my daughter and more thanks to give you, which will all be for nought if we do not flee."

"But you hae your Grail," Duncan broke in. "I'm sorry, wizard, but I dinnae understand. Surely you can use it tae defeat Morgana?"

The wizard looked unhappily at the cup in his hand.

"No, highlander," he said. "I allowed her to control it too. She had my blessing." The wizard clenched his teeth, remembering his own gullibility. "It belongs to her as much as me, and I cannot turn it against her."

He took a deep breath.

"My friends… the situation is far worse than that."

"It can get worse?" Peazle asked incredulously.

"The Grail is glowing." Gorrodin held out the cup, which pulsed with unnatural light. "The Dolorous Stroke has been struck."

The wizard stuffed the cup roughly into his bag, as if he could no longer bear to look at it.

"Come with me to the Thin Place," he said. "I will tell the story as we walk, for it is one you must know.

But gather round close and keep constant watch for danger."

The Clan bunched around the wizard. Gorrodin set off across the valley at a brisk pace, talking as he went.

"Long ago in Galhadria," he said. "There was a terrible civil war. When it was finally over, the greatest sorcerers of the land plotted to make sure it would never happen again…"

"Master Gorrodin, I've… eh… already told them the story of the Dolorous Stroke," Peazle interrupted. "That it means one magical creature has killed another."

"Have you, child?" Gorrodin's bright green eyes darted from place to place, scanning every rock and hollow. "Did you know I added my own small enchantment to the Great Spell?"

The pickpocket shook his head.

"My talisman would begin to glow if ever the Dolorous Stroke took place. A warning of impending doom, you might say."

He stopped. The others were still looking expectantly at him.

"Ah. You do not understand," he said. "It will shine only if the fatal blow was struck by one of my own kind."

"You mean…" Lilly began.

"I mean a Galhadrian has slain one of the Gorrodin Rath." Gorrodin placed a hand gently on his daughter's head. "Though we may escape through a Thin Place, it will only delay the inevitable." He quickened his stride. "Galhadria is doomed."

"The cup began to glow eight months ago," Uallabh said. Lilly shot a startled look at Charlie.

"Wasn't that... around the time you killed Mordred?" she muttered.

"It could not be the boy," Gorrodin cut in. "Excalibur is magical, and they obviously have a bond - but he is only a human."

He squinted at Charlie.

"Unless you have used the Grail to change yourself."

"Not a chance." The boy shook his head.

"He has not, father. I can vouch for that."

Gorrodin allowed himself a resentful sneer.

"Then I suspect Jack Thane's hand in this. He was always too rash, and I imagine he dealt the stoke himself. He may think otherwise, but his arrogance will lead to a war that, ultimately, he cannot win."

"What should we do?"

"What Thane wanted from you in the first place," the wizard said. "We must escape to Galhadria and keep the Grail out of Morgana's hands. Even if we cannot defeat her, it will slow her down and give us some respite. "

"Gorrodin." Peazle pulled at the wizard's bag. "There are children in the valley."

# The Changelings

They looked in the direction the pickpocket was pointing. A crowd of little figures were pouring into the valley, jabbering and singing, heading towards the Clan. All looked thin and malnourished, their hair wild and matted, bodies wrapped in rags. But they scampered across the heather with a skipping run, yelling to each other, like normal youngsters at play.

"Get ready to fight," Gorrodin whispered. "I am weak from my captivity and it will take time to replenish my strength. Yet I may be able to hold them at bay until you reach the safety of the Thin Place."

"No, father!" Lilly whispered, clutching his hand.

"They're just children," Shadowjack grunted. "Not much of an adversary, I'd say."

"They are not children," Gorrodin snapped. "They are Changelings."

Beside the wizard, Duncan bristled.

"What are we dealing with here?" Charlie gripped Excalibur tighter, his palms sweating.

"Galhadrians can be… thoughtless." Gorrodin face was stony as he searched for the right words. "It was worse in days gone by, though I have no time for explanations." He looked towards the laughing crowd.

87

"Occasionally, Galhadrians would bear children in which magic had gone wrong." His expression was still blank, but he could not keep the shame from his voice. "When this happened, the parents would... steal a human baby. Sometimes they would even leave their own in its place."

He was barely whispering now.

"The humans named these impostors Changelings."

"I'd say that was a devil's sight more than thoughtless," Duncan growled, and Gorrodin hung his head.

The children had begun to spread out in a line, still chattering and waving to each other. The Clan kept a wary eye on them.

"Most Changelings were killed by the humans as soon as they realized what had befallen their real offspring," the wizard continued in a contrite tone. "But some escaped to the desolate parts of the highlands, and there they banded together in packs - cursed with a ravenous, never-ending hunger."

"How could they have survived here undetected?"

"Morgana must have locked them away too, to be set upon me, if I was ever released."

"I don't understand." Peazle looked at the mangy children, now standing in a line between the Clan and the Thin Place. "They don't look like much."

"Not until you see their teeth."

Then the row of children opened their mouths, the jaws stretching wider and wider until they seemed to come unhinged. The movement wrinkled up their noses and narrowed their eyes into slits. From each innocent face, two rows of drooling fangs thrust forwards. They roared in unison, a desolate, terrifying ululation that echoed through the valley. It sounded like the end of the world.

Uallabh dropped his pistols and ran.

"Uallabh, no!" Charlie shouted, but the warrior was already sprinting across the heather. The Changelings, seeing the Clan weakened, moved forwards with grotesque prances, surrounding them in a snarling ring.

"Forget him," Duncan snapped, clutching his sword in both hands. "Form a circle facing out, all of you."

Peazle snatched up Uallabh's guns, cocked them and handed one to Lilly. The ring of Changelings began to slowly tighten, as the creatures moved towards them, baring naked fangs.

"Your weapons will do little good against these creatures," Gorrodin said grimly. "Nor a sword made of steel, highlander."

He glanced at Excalibur.

"That will cause some damage, but not enough to save us, I fear."

"I will fight with what I have," Duncan replied and Shadowjack flexed his huge muscles, preparing to defend his friends with bare hands.

"As will I," Gorrodin agreed. But defeat hung heavy in his tone. The wizard ran his fingers tenderly through Lilly's curly hair.

"I am sorry for this, my daughter. All the oceans of this world cannot match the depths of my regret."

Lilly kissed her father's hand and held it against her cheek.

"I will work what defensive magic I can." Gorrodin reached into the bag hanging by his side for his talisman. A look of panic spread across his face.

"The cup is not here!" He rummaged inside the empty satchel. "What treachery is this?"

The Clan looked at each other, equally mystified.

"I took it." Peazle stepped forward. "Not difficult for a pickpocket." He indicated the advancing Changelings, creeping ever closer. "You were all rather... distracted."

"Where is it, boy!?"

"I gave it to Uallabh." Peazle looked at the angry faces all around him. "It was his idea! He said he had a plan!"

The Clan spun round. The warrior was still running, his long red hair streaming behind, growing smaller with every yard he covered. With a start, they realised he was heading for Gorrodin's cave.

The Changelings were looking in the same direction.

Uallabh reached inside his coat and pulled out the Grail. Without breaking stride, he hoisted it above his head. A furious howl rose from the circle of sinister children. As one, they streamed after the fleeing figure.

"No!" Charlie raised his sword and ran after them. With a flying tackle, Duncan brought him crashing to the ground.

"Let him go, Charlie," the highlander urged, lying on top of the struggling boy. "Uallabh is carrying out the oath he swore to Arthur. He is protecting the Grail."

The Changelings caught the fleeing warrior as he reached the mouth of the cave. Charlie's last sight of his friend was a tiny figure covered in clawing, biting creatures, disappearing into the crevasse. His final roar drifted out of the darkness, as the last of the Changelings poured into the mountain after him.

"Nimve!" he cried with his dying breath. The cup came flying out of the closing gap and landed on the grass.

There was a shuddering sigh, and the two sides of the cliff face swung shut. Charlie clapped both hands over his eyes to blot out the sight. The rest looked on, stunned.

"We are safe." Gorrodin's voice was a hoarse whisper. "But the cost was high, indeed."

"We made him leave his coffin behind," Shadowjack said, to no one in particular.

Peazle stood apart from the rest, shaking uncontrollably.

"I didn't know," he whispered. "I didn't know he was going to do *that*."

Shadowjack put his arm around the trembling boy while Lilly fetched the Grail. Duncan stood and pulled Charlie roughly to his feet.

"I was wrong to doubt him," the highlander said quietly. "He was a fine warrior and a good man."

He tried to sound tough but his voice was uneven and his hands shook.

"Look!" Lilly indicated a nearby hillock.

A tall figure was striding towards them, a bowler hat under one arm. The stranger was covered in mud and tufts of heather – but under the grime, he appeared to be wearing a suit and raincoat. Duncan's sword was raised in a flash and the rest of the Clan tensed to attack, their desperation replaced by anger.

"Hey, I'm one of the good guys." The man one hand in surrender. "My name is Inspector Archer of Birmingham CID."

"Nice to meet you," Peazle said. "I see you have my hat."

The Clan sat on a grassy hill beside the Thin Place. They had told Inspector Archer their story and the policeman looked suitably stunned.

"What will you do now?" he asked the seated figures.

"With the Grail in my possession, Morgana no longer has any reason to pursue Charlie," the wizard replied. "You may take him home, Archer. I gather that is why you are here."

"What *will* Morgana do?"

"She will rally her army in Toth and prepare for war. Even without the cup, they are a mighty force, and the Dolorous Stroke means they will surely win."

Gorrodin smiled wanly at the others.

"The rest of you are free as well. You may return to Galhadria or stay on earth. You choose."

"I'll stay," Duncan said fiercely. "The devil himself couldnae find me in these hills, and I am done with Jack Thane."

"What about you, wizard?" Peazle asked.

"I shall go to Galhadria. The Lords will not welcome me, but they shall need my help in the battle that will soon come." Gorrodin looked fondly at Lilly. "First, I would have a little time to know my child again."

The rest nodded, understanding. Charlie looked at Gorrodin, arm still round his daughter, then at the Inspector. Archer caught the glance.

"God knows how we're going to explain this to your parents," he said. Charlie's hair was matted with blood and dirt, and his clothes were in shreds. "Better start thinking up a good excuse."

He reached out his hand to the boy.

Charlie blinked hard. The rest of the group got up and gathered awkwardly around him, not knowing what to say. The boy choked back a sob and straightened his shoulders.

"Where are *you* going, Peazle?"

"To Galhadria," Peazle said. "I shall help Gorrodin prepare for war against Morgana. For all the Lord's faults, their home is my home now."

"Then take this." Charlie handed over Excalibur. "I won't be needing it anymore."

"I will go with you, Peazle," Shadowjack said. "I doubt there's much work here for blacksmiths these days.

They both looked round at Duncan.

"Ach, so will I," the highlander sighed. "You'd be lost without me and fighting is what I know best."

"Naturally, I will accompany my father," Lilly said.

"I hae a brother," Duncan turned to the Inspector. "He went missing when he was just a baby. I've not found him so far."

Inspector Archer looked at the spot where the Changelings had been trapped. He reached out and shook the highlander's hand.

"I'll keep my eyes open."

"Then let us depart.

"Wait." Peazle looked ashamed. "Before we leave, there is something I must tell you."

His face had gone bright red.

"I have kept it to myself and had no intention of carrying it out. But I fear it may be important."

The rest of the group looked at him quizzically.

"I was given a secret mission by Jack Thane." Peazle sat down on a rock. "And I have the horrible feeling it was the real reason he sent a former pick-pocket to find Charlie."

"Out with it, young man," Gorrodin commanded.

"I was told to steal a silver bear on a chain around his neck and give it to Thane."

Gorrodin went white.

"A silver bear?" he repeated quietly. "That cannot be."

"I'm afraid it can."

The voice came from behind them. Charlie whirled round, recognising it immediately.

"*Mum*?"

"Hello, my boy. I cannot tell you how delighted I am to see you."

Charlie's mother and father stood, a few feet away, as if they had appeared from nowhere.

.

# The Silver Bear

"Mum!" Charlie ran over and squeezed the woman. "I'm sorry! You must have been so worried."

He turned awkwardly to his dad.

"I have a good excuse, I promise."

"I don't doubt it." His father hugged him. "And it's us who should apologise."

"What? *Why*?"

"We have been in hiding for a long, long time." His mother said sadly. "And now you have become the victim of our deception."

"I don't understand." Charlie looked at his parents, but they were staring at Gorrodin.

"I never thought to set eyes on you both again," the Wizard smiled.

"Wait." Charlie felt like his head might explode. "You know each other?"

"Very well." Gorrodin strode forwards and threw his arms around Charlie's mum. "This is my sister Ganieda, one of the Lords of the Western Wilderness."

He released the woman and clasped Charlie's father by the hand.

"Words cannot express how glad I am to set eyes on you again, my liege."

"My *liege*." Charlie almost fell over. "That's my father."

"Is it, now?" Gorrodin regarded the boy with something approaching awe. "I know him by another name."

He gave a small smile.

"This is the great warrior king, Arthur."

"Just hold on a minute!" the boy stammered. "I saw Arthur when I drank the potion Peazle gave me. He didn't look anything like dad!"

"A potion Peazle got from Jack Thane," his mother replied grimly. "I'm sure he added his own little enchantment to make sure you did not recognise your father and discover your true lineage."

"Why would he do that?"

"Using people is Jack's speciality," Charlie's mum said. "Which is always easier if he keeps vital information from them."

There was a stunned silence from the rest of the group. Finally, Peazle knelt, taking off his bowler.

"I am at your service, my liege."

The rest followed suit.

"My dad is King Arthur, and my mum is one of the Little People," Charlie muttered. "I'm finding this all a bit difficult to take in."

"Sit, all of you." Charlie's mum plonked herself on a flat stone. "My boy deserves to hear the truth about us, and the rest of you must know it too."

They dutifully sat.

"I have hidden my powers for longer than I can remember," she said sadly. "Concealed my talisman, so none could ever find me. Never thought I would need it again, but that time of innocence is obviously over."

She held out her hand to Charlie.

"May I have it back for a while?"

"Here." The boy pulled the chain over his head and handed the silver bear to her.

"I will return it in due course for, as my heir, I bestowed it upon you." She cupped the talisman in her hand.

"You sound different, mum," Charlie said anxiously.

"I love you with all my soul," the woman replied. "But please refer to me as Ganieda or my Lady, from now on."

"*Seriously?*"

"Where we're going, mum doesn't sound powerful enough." She winked at him. "And I must assert myself with the other wizards of Galhadria. So, I better get used to their stuffy way of talking again."

"You are coming with us?" Gorrodin asked.

"We are. For the fate of both worlds hangs in the balance."

She waved a hand in the air.

"But first, you must know our story."

"Go on then," Charlie said. "It might help me get my head round the fact that my mother is a sorceress and my father is King bloody Arthur."

Sparks flew from Ganieda's fingertips and the Clan watched as a picture formed in the air.

*Arthur lay dying on the battlefield. Clustered around him were his few surviving knights: Lucan, Bedivere, Griflet, and Blioberis. Morgana and the remaining Gorrodin Rath had fled, and the battlefield was awash with blood and bodies.*

*"My king's wounds are too severe for him to live much longer." Lucan shook his head miserably. "The Round Table is no more."*

*"This need not be so." A woman appeared beside them, dressed in an emerald dress. "My name is Ganieda and I shall tend to his injuries."*

*She placed slim hands on the gaping wound splitting Arthur's chest and a strange glow emanated from her fingers. Slowly the gash began to heal.*

*"You are Galhadrian," Griflet gasped. "Like Gorrodin, Arthur's old advisor."*

*"Why did your people not aid us when we needed you most?" Lucan spat. "We thought ourselves your allies."*

*"I stood by and watched when they banished my brother, Gorrodin," Ganieda replied bitterly. "Now he is imprisoned and I do not know where."*

*She bowed her head.*

*"And yes, we did nothing when you were slaughtered fighting a race that will become our enemies too."*

*She stood and waved her arm. A glowing blue circle appeared a few yards away.*

*"I am done with my people," she said defiantly. "Belvedere, gather all the silver and use it to block up the tunnels where the remaining Gorrodin Rath hide. I shall take Arthur to a place of safety."*

*"Thank you, my Lady."*

*"It is I who should thank you. I shall shield my talisman, remain in the world of men and the Lords of the Western Wilderness will never find me."*

*She picked up Arthur as if he were feather light, stepped through the portal and vanished.*

"I tended to Arthur until he was fit and well and, in the process, we fell in love." Ganieda glanced at her husband, who blew her a kiss.

"Oh, please don't do that," Charlie blushed.

"Had I any thoughts of returning to Galhadria, they were gone."

"Ganiedia's magic kept me young," Arthur said. "We changed our names and travelled the world for centuries, with no plans other than to live our lives in peace."

His wife's face clouded.

"The Lords of the Western Wilderness *did* have plans, however." She waved her hand again. "They always do."

Now the Clan were transported to Galhadria, where Jack Thane was addressing the other wizards.

*"We made a grievous error in allowing Arthur's knights to be destroyed," he said. "It prompted Ganieda to leave us and we cannot locate her."*

*"Then we will do without," Tom Lincoln shrugged. "We are weakened but no one dare challenge us."*

*"There will always be potential enemies on our borders," Thane countered. "Yet we cannot subdue them without risking the Dolorous Stroke."*

*"Do you have a solution?"*

*"Yes. We will resurrect the Round Table."*

*"That will be a feat, indeed," Mabon scoffed. "There are only a handful left."*

*"Arthur was sometimes called The Knight With 1,000 Eyes," Thane countered. "Do you know why?"*

*"We have no interest in human gossip."*

*"Because he sent 500 of his most upright warriors far and wide. They were dispatched to do good deeds and fight oppression wherever they went."*

*"That is noble, if rather pointless," Math said. "What of it?"*

*"It was brilliant," Thane sighed. "On one hand, it ensured that Arthur was known and revered in the most far-flung lands. And it also showed his strength. If he could afford to send his finest men so far from home, how mighty must his kingdom be?"*

"So, he was a fairly able tactician," Prestor John shrugged. "What use is that to us?"

"When the Round Table was destroyed, the 1,000 Eyes saw no point in returning. Instead, they settled where they were and raised families of their own."

"I begin to see what you are getting at," Math said.

"Suppose we were to… take descendants of these knights to Galhadria? Raise them to be mighty warriors from birth?" Thane paused to let the idea sink in. "We can send them to Alabarra, The Wooded Kingdom and Monshorn. Anywhere that potential enemies might lurk. There, they can perform the same function for Galhadria as they did on earth."

"That is very clever."

"They will roam the wilderness, dispatching our foes and earning the gratitude of the inhabitants. And, because they are not magical, there will be no Dolorous Stroke."

He tapped his chin slyly.

"If one knight should be killed, we will simply replace him with another."

"That is a shrewd idea indeed," Tom Lincoln chuckled. "Let us put it to the vote."

Every one of the Lords raised their hands.


"The wizards *did* take my brother," Duncan cried. "And then lied tae me about it!"

He looked angrily at Charlie's mum.

"Could ye no have done something?"

"I have been in hiding for centuries," Ganieda shook her head. "Even if I had not left, I would have been outvoted and powerless to stop it."

Her eyes glinted with steely resolve.

"But things have changed. My own brother is free again, and the Lords are in dire straits. They need us. That gives us leverage."

She laid a hand on Duncan's arm.

"I will unite you with your brother. You have my word."

"I will hold ye to that."

"What about Charlie?" Peazle asked. "Where did he come into your plans?"

"My wife and I have always been happy with each other," Arthur said. "But, eventually, our lives felt incomplete."

"So we had a child," Ganieda finished his sentence. "Who we love dearly."

"And who is half Galhadrian." Gorrodin paled. "A magical creature."

"Why, thanks," Charlie blushed. "But I don't have any spell casting abilities. I must take after my dad."

"It doesn't matter." Lilly put a hand to her mouth. "You killed Mordred."

"Who was also a magical creature." Gorrodin clasped his hands together.

"Charlie. It was *you* who delivered the Dolorous Stroke and doomed Galhadria."

# Castle Alclud

"How was I to know?" the boy objected. "Honestly, I get the blame for everything."

"Nobody is blaming you, son," Arthur assured him. "The fault is ours for hiding your lineage."

"We just wanted you to have a normal life," Ganieda said. "It did not work out quite the way we'd hoped."

"You *think*?"

"Galhadria may be condemned but I'm going to fight for it, anyway." Duncan stuck out his chest. "It's the only way to find my brother."

"Speak for yourself," Peazle frowned. "I'm certainly having second thoughts now."

"The Lords are a rum bunch, I'll agree," Shadowjack rumbled. "But the common folk of Galhadria always treated me well. I cannot stand by and let them die."

"You don't understand," Ganieda snapped. "Jack Thane has no honour or scruples. I am sure he has thought of a plan to achieve victory."

"That's good, isn't it?" Charlie asked. "What do you suppose he intends to do?"

"All I know is that he was desperate to get his hands on your cup, brother." His mother held up the silver bear. "And my talisman too."

She turned to Peazle.

"He asked you to steal it for him, did he not?"

"He did." The boy went red.

"Either would greatly increase the Lords' power." The wizard tapped his long nose. "But nothing can break the Great Spell. The Dolorous Stroke means the Gorrodin Rath cannot lose."

"Then, why did Thane want our talismans so badly, if they would do him no good in battle?"

"I have no idea."

"Nor I. And the only way I can find out his scheme is to go to Galhadria with you."

Inspector Archer coughed loudly and they all stared at him.

"Can I come too?" he asked. "This seems like a once in a lifetime experience, plus I've still got a few days of paid vacation left."

"Ye certainly may." Duncan clapped him on the back. "Do you have a sword?"

"Sorry, no."

"Nae matter. We'll pick something up when we get there. Are ye right or left-handed?"

"Does it matter?"

"I dinnae suppose so."

"When we arrive, follow my lead," Gorrodin commanded. "No matter what may transpire."

He clapped thin hands and a misty blue glow spread across the top of the hillock.

Jack Thane faced the rest of the Lords in the Whale Room. Each one regarded him stonily.

"The Gorrodin Rath will attack any day now," Baubi Ross said. "You have run out of time to deliver on your grand promises."

Thane shuffled from foot to foot.

"There has been a delay…" he began.

"You have nothing!" Tom Lincoln snapped. "If we did not need you to help us fight, you would be in chains right now."

"I have recalled the Round Table from the far-flung corners of our lands. They are formidable fighters."

"That will do no good!"

"I… Eh…" For once, Thane was lost for words.

A shimmering glow appeared in the corner of the room. As the Lords gaped, Gorrodin and Ganieda stepped through, followed by Arthur, Peazle, Duncan, Shadowjack, Charlie, Lilly and Inspector Archer.

Jack Thane recovered quickly.

"I believe reinforcements have arrived."

Jenny Haa and Will Thorn were on their feet in an instant.

"You dare invade our hall, Gorrodin. You have been banished."

"Nor are *you* welcome, Ganieda," Prestor John spat. "You deserted us long ago, for some human."

"You will address my wife as *Mistress* Ganieda."
Charlie's dad stepped forwards, calm and collected.
"And refer to me as King Arthur of Taneborc."

"Arthur. The Knight With 1,000 Eyes." Jack Thane
bowed to him. "Welcome, Sire."

"We are here to help in any way we can," Gorrodin
said. "We would not desert Galhadria in its hour of
need, and I imagine you could do with our assistance."

"I strongly suggest we let bygones be bygones."
Jack Thane smiled disarmingly. "I require either Gorrodin's cup or Mistress Ganieda's talisman to ensure
victory. Having both is even better."

He bowed to them as well.

"I presume you have brought the bear and the cup?"

"We didn't get here on a flying carpet."

"Then I welcome you," Lincoln said brusquely.
"For beggars cannot be choosers."

He pointed at Jack Thane.

"I will know your strategy, right now, and brook no
more secrecy or delay."

"Of course, Master Lincoln." The wizard beckoned
to Charlie and the boy trotted forwards.

"This is Charlie Wilson, son of Mistress Ganieda
and King Arthur. As such, he is half Galhadrian."

"Pleased to meet you, I think."

The Lords looked far from pleased.

"It was this boy who killed Mordred, son of Morgana and so delivered the Dolorous Stroke."

The Lord's demeanour passed from outrage to outright hostility.

"You have given us the cause but not the solution," Will Thorn shouted. "This changes nothing."

"Charlie Wilson is also half-human." Thane smiled slyly. "Which means there are *two* races the Gorrodin Rath are certain to defeat in any war."

"I begin to understand." As always, Math was quickest to catch on. "With Gorrodin's cup and Ganiedia's bear, we are back to our former strength."

"So it will take the Gorrodin Rath a little longer to defeat us," Prestor John fumed.

"We would have enough power to open up all the thin places to earth again." Thane countered. "Combine them in front of the Great Wall, just as the enemy reach it."

"Of course!" Mabon breathed. "The Gorrodin Rath would never reach Galhadria. They'd be transported all over earth instead!"

"Then we shut the Thin Places again, forever this time." Mabon clasped her hands. "Morgana and her race will conquer humanity instead, and we will be saved."

The Clan stared at the Lords in horror. Yet, before they could voice their opposition, Ganieda spoke.

"That is an excellent plan," she said. "I commend you master Thane."

"You're welcome." But the wizard looked suspicious. "I thought you might object, having lived there so long."

"I only care that my family is safe." The woman did not bat an eyelid. "In return for our help, Gorrodin and I wish to be returned to our rightful places with the Lords and would ask that our children be welcomed as well."

There were mutterings from the gathered sorcerers.

"I shall reluctantly grant that," Lincoln replied. "And who is this?"

He scowled at Inspector Archer.

"My son's protector. He stays too."

"Agreed."

"I have a request as well." Arthur stepped forwards. "I wish to be put in charge of your army."

"That is a step too far," Lincoln growled. "We do not know you."

"You know my reputation," the man said coolly. "I have fought in countless wars throughout human history. When was the last time you engaged in battle?"

Charlie goggled his father. He no longer bore any resemblance to the man he had known all his life.

"If Thane's plan works, you will have no need of me," Arthur continued. "If something goes wrong, however, you will wish you had granted my boon."

"I see sense in that." Math nodded. "And this is no time for misplaced vanity."

"I shall let it be known that you will command our forces," Lincoln sighed. "Is that it?"

"Let us not call our foe the Gorrodin Rath anymore," Gorrodin spoke up. "For they have long abandoned my guidance. The Rath will do."

"I have no problem granting that wish."

"Then, I would like to retire with my party." Ganieda yawned. "The last few days have been quite an ordeal for us all."

"And I would spend some time with my daughter," Gorrodin added. "We have many lost years to catch up on."

"Very well." Lincoln held out his hand. "Give me your talismans. We will place them in the spell chamber with our own."

Ganieda slipped the chain over her head and surrendered the silver bear. Gorrodin hesitated, then passed over his cup.

"It is done." Tom Lincoln signalled the meeting was adjourned "When the Rath attack, we will open up the Thin Places together and link them in front of the Great Wall."

"I fear it is our kingdom Morgana wants most," Prester John warned. "She will try to prevent them going through."

"When their bloodlust is up, even Morgana will not be able to stop the Rath." For the first time in weeks, Tom Lincoln smiled.

"We are saved."

# The Decision

The Clan were escorted to their rooms by a blue-coated attendant. As soon as he was gone, Duncan rounded on his companions.

"I cannae believe that…" he began angrily.

Lilly put a finger to her lips until he calmed down.

They waited while Gorrodin weaved a spell of silence to ward off prying ears.

"We cannot let this happen," Lilly said finally. "The human race has many flaws but they do not deserve such a fate."

"Neither do the Galhadrians," Gorrodin replied. "I fear we are stuck between a rock and a hard place."

"The Lord's plan is truly abominable," Shadowjack grumbled. "Though I have to say, it's pretty ingenious too."

"We have been outmanoeuvred." Ganieda slumped in a chair. "Unsealing a Thin Place takes great power. With our talismans, my brother and I might have managed to open one right here and let us escape back to earth. Now we no longer possess them."

She looked lost.

"We have no choice. We must save Galhadria."

There was a chorus of objections from the rest of the Clan.

"Mum?" Charlie pleaded. "You don't have to help Thane. You could sabotage his plan by not taking part."

"Do you not understand?" his mother sighed. "We are stuck here. If we do not aid the Lords, the Rath will destroy us all."

She laid a tired hand on his shoulder.

"I will not let you die, no matter what the cost."

"That's no your decision tae make," Duncan shot back.

"I'm truly sorry, but nothing can change my mind."

"Remember what you told me?" Charlie looked at his father. "Sometimes virtue is its own reward."

"I also told you that wearing glasses would make your eyes recede into your head."

"Don't be flippant, dad. You must recall what else you said."

"There are two great virtues a person can have." Arthur straightened his shoulders. "Knowing what is right and doing what is right."

He kissed his wife on the top of her head.

"The Lords cast the Great Spell and Galhadria is prepared for war. Humanity is not. Though they will lose, it is *this* land where the battle should be fought."

"I agree with Lord Arthur," Gorrodin nodded. "I usually do."

"Arthur, no!" his wife cried. "Our son!"

"I will have two of my new knights escort him to the farthest corner of the realm."

He indicated the rest of the Clan.

"You can go with him, if that is your desire."

"I dinnae run from danger," Duncan said angrily. "I will fight."

"I'll stick around too," Shadowjack raised his hand.

"And me," Peazle sighed.

"I may as well stay," Inspector Archer said. "I don't really know my way around."

"My daughter will accompany you, Charlie." Gorrodin sounded relieved.

"Lilly shall do no such thing." The girl stamped her foot. "I will not abandon my friends."

"Or me." Charlie hugged his mother. "I appreciate what you're doing, but I am the son of King Arthur. He was willing to give his life fighting the Rath once before. I can do no less."

"He's picking up Galhadrian speak quite well," Arthur remarked.

"You joke at a time like this?" Ganieda shot him a filthy look, but Arthur held her stare.

"I agree that humanity has many flaws. Sacrificing themselves to do what is right is not one of them."

His eyes took on a hard spark.

"This is something your Lords have obviously forgotten."

"Surely humanity cannot lose," Peazle piped up. "The Rath army is great, but humans number in their millions. They have weapons now the enemy cannot conceive of."

"The Rath also have a secret weapon," Arthur replied. "It was part of the enchantment they wove for themselves, long ago. Why do you imagine there are so many of them? Why are the Galhadrian forces still heavily armoured with fairy silver, as my knights once were?"

"I think I can guess," Peazle gulped. "The Rath do not breed, do they? They have another way of reproducing."

"Yes. The creatures' bites are infectious and will turn anyone on the receiving end into one of them. Let a few of them loose in a human city and Morgana will have another army within hours. A scenario that will be duplicated all over earth."

Peazle caught on first.

"The Rath did not wipe out the inhabitants of Toth. They *turned* them."

"You're kidding," Charlie stammered. "Like in a zombie film?"

"Exactly."

"If we allow Jack Thane's plan to go ahead," Gorrodin said. "He will be seen as Galhadria's saviour and, most likely, its ruler. Is that something you could accept, Ganieda? He is as bad as Morgana."

"If the Rath took Galhadria, how long would it be before they moved on Alabarra, The Wooded Kingdom, Monshorn and then lands beyond?" Ganieda looked pleadingly at her brother. "Turned the inhabitants into monsters? Even if they fled, our children would never be safe."

Gorrodin was silent for a long time.

"You are right," he said finally. "We have no choice but to go along with Thane's plan."

There was a chorus of objections from the Clan.

"Enough!" Gorrodin raised a fist, crackling with light. "It is decided. Return to your rooms."

Arthur said nothing, but his lips tightened.

The Clan were awakened at dawn by bells ringing.

"The Gorrodin Rath are massing to attack." The blue-coated attendant ran from door to door. "Morgana herself has been sighted."

The occupants stumbled into the corridor.

"I thought they would come at night." Shadowjack rubbed sleep from his eyes. "I was dreaming about being on a pirate ship and only having one leg."

"It is a fear tactic," Arthur replied. "They are no longer repelled by the sun and wish the Galhadrians to fully understand their increased power."

He grabbed the attendant.

"Bring silver armour for my companions and me, then lead us to my knights."

500 mounted men were stretched out on the plain behind the Great Wall, sunlight glinting off their breastplates and helmets. Behind them were massed

ranks of armed Galhadrians. Charlie estimated there were upwards of 5,000 fighters.

On the hill above, Castle Alclud towered above the army.

"Quite a formidable array." Duncan looked impressed. "I doubted there would be so many."

"I'll wager they were never told the Dolorous Stroke had been struck," Gorrodin said. "They think they have a chance at winning. Even if they were aware of the true situation, however, I dare say they would fight to the last man to defend their land."

"Yet, not one of them are trained for battle," Arthur grunted. "They have not fought a war in centuries."

"They won't have to, will they?" Charlie remarked sourly. "The Rath will never reach the wall."

"Gorrodin and I must go to the spell chamber and prepare." Ganieda kissed her son's head and glanced at her husband. "I hope, someday, you will both forgive me."

"I would ask a small spell from each of you before you go," Arthur asked. "Gorrodin, can you amplify my voice so the troops can all hear me?"

The wizard snapped his fingers.

"It is done."

"And I want to know which of these knights is Duncan's brother."

Ganieda pressed a palm to her forehead, scanning the ranks in an instant.

"Front row, second from the left," she said. "There is a man who looks just like him."

"They're all wearing helmets."

"I'm a sorceress, aren't I?" She beckoned to Gorrodin. "Let us not put off this sorry spectacle any further, brother."

She clapped her hands, and the pair vanished.

"Off you go, lad," Arthur said. "We will wait for our steeds."

"Steeds?" Charlie looked horrified. "I've never sat on a horse in my life. The closest I ever got was a donkey on Brighton beach."

"Can't say I've been on one either," Inspector Archer added. "Never fancied being in the mounted police. Those buggers have teeth like paving stones, and that's just the riders."

"I can provide better transportation." Peazle pointed to a small copse of trees at the edge of the valley. "It's stashed over there."

He bowed to Arthur.

"With your permission, my king."

"Every little helps, as they say at Tesco's."

"I've no idea what that meant, but I'll go get it."

He took off at a run.


Duncan reached the ranks of knights and stopped in front of the one Ganieda had picked out. Now that the moment he had waited for so long had arrived, he had no idea how to proceed.

"Hello, Caleb," he said, finally. "You've grown up a wee bit."

The knight removed his helmet, revealing a shock of ginger hair.

"Oh." Duncan was taken aback. "You definitely take after oor father's line. He had a head like an orange thistle."

"My name is Sir Galahad, not Caleb." The man looked puzzled. "Sorry, but do I know you?"

"You do not," Duncan sat. "It is a long story, and this is not the time tea tell it." He paused.

"You are my brother."

"Of course. We are all brothers here."

"No. Though, I cannae prove it, I am your flesh and blood. Your real brother."

"You look just like me, apart from that dark hair." The man hesitated. "I don't understand."

"Explanations will have tae wait." Duncan stepped forward and laid a hand on Galahad's leg. "Just know that I have searched for you for centuries and prayed for this moment."

The man looked into Duncan's eyes.

"Then I believe you. Brother."

"Those are words I have longed tae hear for longer than I can remember."

"Your timing could be better, however."

"Dinnae get me started on that."

"Stay close and I will defend you." The man leant down and clasped Duncan's hand. "When this is over, I will seek you out. We have much to talk about."

"That we do." Duncan let go and marched back to his companions, wiping tears from his eyes.


The attendant had arrived with a group of white horses. Shadowjack heaved himself onto a charger.

"Sorry, beastie," he apologised. "I must be quite a weight to carry. I've not bothered with a helmet, or else your legs might collapse."

Duncan arrived.

"I am ready." He leapt onto his steed in a single bound.

There was a throbbing hum and Peazle appeared over a rise.

"Is that an… armoured car?" Charlie gasped.

The boy drew up alongside them and switched off the engine.

"This is a Patria AMV XP personnel carrier," he said proudly. "Armour plated with a 12.7 mm machine gun, 30 mm cannon, 7.62 mm coaxial machine gun and two guided anti-tank heat-seeking missile launchers. Plus, it's filled with automatic weapons."

He jumped out and patted the sides.

"Jack Thane turned the whole thing silver to pack an added punch against the Rath." He shrugged. "He does like his modern toys, though the other Lords frown upon his collection and made him stop."

He shrugged.

"So I hid this wee beauty from them."

"Where the hell did you get it?"

"Stole it from an army base in Finland. There's still a Thin Place open there, so I drove it through."

"I'll be getting in that for sure," Lilly clambered up the side, Inspector Archer right behind.

"What's the point?" Charlie protested. "We're not actually going to fight."

"Your father is King Arthur." Lilly peered down at him. "You honestly think he's not going to do what he believes is right?"

"Dad?" Charlie looked up at the mounted man.

"I intend leading my forces to war." Arthur nodded sadly. "You must take the carrier in the opposite direction, for we are sure to be defeated."

"But I can't lose you!"

"Fate has played its hand, boy. I will meet my end happily if you stay alive."

"I love you, Dad." Charlie climbed into the armoured vehicle. "Please don't die."

"I shall do my best."

Arthur took a deep breath, then addressed his troops.

"I am your commander, Arthur of Taneborc." His voice rang loudly and clearly through the valley. "The Rath are about to attack and, normally, I would line the Great Wall with archers, for it *seems* an impenetrable barrier. But Morgana is leading them and she is no fool.

Therefore, I must assume she has a way to bring the barrier down."

There was a collective gasp from the assembled army.

"If she does, we will be at a grave disadvantage. The Rath will scramble over the rubble in their thousands and our cavalry will be useless, with no room to manoeuvre. They will be forced to dismount and fight on foot."

A few of the knights nodded, understanding their limitations in such a situation.

"Therefore, we will do the last thing Morgana expects. We shall attack first." He raised his hand. "Open the gates and reform on the other side of the wall."

The attendants stared at him. But he was the leader of their forces. Reluctantly they unbarred and swung open the huge gates.

Arthur's army marched through and began to take up their places.

Inside the armoured carrier, Peazle turned to his companions.

"What is it to be, folks?" he asked. "Fight or flee?"

"I'm not leaving mum and dad." Charlie folded his arms. "I just can't do it."

"I'm a policeman," Inspector Archer rubbed his bald head. "My job is to take on bad guys. And I know how to drive."

"Looks like we're staying," Lilly said. "I'll man the cannon."

"I shall take the machine gun," Peazle grinned wryly. "Wish I'd stolen a helmet too. This bowler hat isn't going to be much protection."

The armoured carrier roared to life and rumbled after the Galhadrians. Arthur swung round on his mount when he heard the commotion.

"Aw, no, you little fool," he groaned. "You could have gotten away."

But it was too late. The gates swung shut behind them and were barred.

# Betrayal

Gorrodin and Ganieda wound down stone steps to the spell room, where the Lord's talismans were kept. As the most precious artefacts in Galhadria, they were locked away in the deepest dungeons of Castle Alclud and closely guarded. An attendant unlocked a heavy wooden door, protected by magic, no doubt. The spell room was small, with ancient stone walls devoid of windows. The other sorcerers were gathered around plinths, each holding their most precious objects.

"Are you both ready?" Math urged.

"We are."

The pair took their places and placed their hands on the silver bear and the Grail cup.

"The Rath have gathered," Tom Lincoln said. "They have no patience and, therefore, an attack is imminent."

"When they charge, we will cast our spell on my signal," Jack Thane said. "I have calculated the exact location to open the giant portal in front of the wall."

"It must be timed to perfection," Prestor John added. "They will cross the valley floor at a run, and they are fast."

"Then let us prepare." Lincoln bent over his talisman, a long clay pipe. "This will take our utmost concentration and skill."

The pipe began to softly vibrate.

"How will we know when the Rath move?" Ganieda interrupted. "When we are concentrating all our powers down here."

"There is a watcher on the wall." Jack Thane held up a walkie talkie. "An acquisition from your young friend, Peazle, on one of his forays."

Tom Lincoln tutted his displeasure, but the rest held their tongues.

"So you found humans are good for something, eh, Master Thane?" Gorrodin grunted.

"I have no desire to destroy the kingdom of men and I grieve for what will happen," Thane replied defiantly. "But it is them or us. Now focus."

The Lords bent over their talismans and, one by one, each began to radiate with soft light. As if on cue, the radio crackled to life.

*An attack has begun, Master Thane.*

"We are ready. Let us know when the Rath are moments from the wall."

*I do not understand*, the voice fizzed back. *It is our side who are advancing. Was it not at your command?*

Tom Lincoln's eyes widened. He swept his arm in an arc and the pipe before him faded.

A vision appeared in the air. They could see the Galhadrian army spreading out slowly across the plane of Toth, Arthur and his knights in front.

"What is this treachery?" Thane gasped. "They are in the way! There is nowhere for us to open the portal."

The Lords broke into a panicked babble, and Thane rounded on Ganieda and Gorrodin.

"You have betrayed us," he spat. "I will have you thrown into our deepest pit for eternity."

"We knew nothing of this." Gorrodin put a hand on his chest. "Use enchantment to look into our hearts if you doubt it."

"This was not my doing." Ganieda had turned pale. "I swear."

"Our forces are under the command of your husband!"

"My husband, not me!" the woman retorted. "Do you think I would knowingly put my own son in the firing line?"

"I say we lock them up," Prestor John grunted. "Who knows what other mischief they will cause?"

"Do not let your anger overcome common sense," Ganieda retorted. "You are going to need us for the coming fight."

"A fight we cannot win!"

"You'll lose a damned sight faster if Gorrodin and I are locked up," Ganieda retorted. "Arthur has taken command of the army and gone against my wishes. Now I see no course of action but to support him."

"This is a coup," Thane roared. "Do not listen to them."

"It's no coup. It's the opportunity to regain the honour you obviously lost long ago." Ganieda's voice was laden with sorrow. "My husband has determined this war will be waged honestly, and he and my son shall lose their lives because of it."

"Well spoken, sister," Gorrodin said. "Arthur has forged his own path. Like it or not, we must follow where he leads."

The Lords looked at Tom Lincoln. The wizard's mouth worked silently as he struggled to contain his rage.

"You cannot allow…" Thane began.

"Enough!" Lincoln shouted. "There is no more time for debate. Let us make haste to the Great Wall."

He picked up his talisman.

"We will show these traitors we know how to die with dignity."

# Part 3

The Great Battle

*"This is beyond understanding." said the king. "You are the wisest man alive. You know what is preparing. Why do you not make a plan to save yourself?"*

*And Merlin said quietly, "Because I am wise. In the combat between wisdom and feeling, wisdom never wins."*

John Steinbeck. *The Acts of King Arthur and His Noble Knights.*

# Toth-Haden

Tom Lincoln and the other wizards materialised on top of the Great Wall. Below them, the two armies faced each other.

"Where are our archers?" Mabon demanded. "This is the perfect vantage point to fire down on the enemy."

"Grouped at the back of the troops below." Mabon pointed down. "This Arthur is an incompetent fool!"

"He is a brilliant general," Gorrodin countered. "If there are no defenders up here, it is for a reason."

"What possible reason could he have?"

"Think!" Ganieda snapped. "Morgana did not know about your plan to open a portal. Why would she send her minions against a barrier they cannot breach?"

"She would not," Gorrodin concluded. "Therefore, she must have a way to bring down the wall."

"Impossible!" Tom Lincoln laughed. "It is reinforced with our magic. Even if she had the Grail, Morgana's powers would never be strong enough to raze this mighty structure."

He slammed his hand against a stone nacelle.

"Because of Arthur, the Rath will wipe out our forces without having to even tackle it."

"He has a point." Gorrodin glanced at Ganieda.

"Arthur knows he must lose," she replied. "But he would never throw away the lives of those he commands to make a point. He's far too clever for that."

"I agree." Gorrodin turned to the other Lords. "I trust my king. My sister and I will fight below. You are fools if you stay here."

The siblings stepped off the parapet and floated down, cloaks flapping in the wind. They soared across the Galhadrians and landed beside Arthur.

"Hello, dear. Sorry about this."

"Hi, mum." Charlie waved from the top of the armoured carrier. Ganieda gave an agonised groan.

"Stay out of the fighting," she commanded. "Or else."

"Bit late now."

"If we survive, you and I shall be having serious words," she rasped at her husband. "You allowed our son to come with you!"

"It seems I'm not the only one who won't do as he's told," the king faltered. "I did not think…"

"You never do." Ganieda turned on her heel and walked towards her son, casting a hate-filled look at Arthur. "I'll never forgive you."

Arthur blinked back tears. Charlie was about to climb down, in a vain attempt to smooth things over, when a shadow fell across the valley.

"Oh, my stars." Gorrodin looked up.

"It *can't* be."

A gigantic shape rose over the mountains, filling the sky. It was twice the size of a jumbo jet, kept in the air by wings that stretched the width of the valley.

"What the hell is that beastie?" Duncan whispered.

"Toth-Haden." Gorrodin's voice shook. "The greatest of the Black Dragons – a race that was supposed to have died out millennia ago."

"I presume he's bad news," Arthur shielded his eyes with one hand.

"It's a female. And she could annihilate half your army with one blast of her fiery breath."

"I'll take that as a yes." The king raised one arm and motioned for his men to move slowly forwards.

"You're going to attack now?" Shadowjack's eyes were on stalks. "After what the wizard just told you."

"I'm moving my forces away from the wall," Arthur replied. "For that will surely be her first target. Thank God the Lords are up there to defend it."

"Dragon magic is the most powerful kind ever discovered." Gorrodin shook his head. "They cannot hope to match it, though I fear they will try."

Toth-Haden flapped her wings and moved swiftly towards the Great Wall. Tom Lincoln and his fellow wizards launched a dozen bolts of lightning at her, but they simply bounced off the scaly black hide.

The dragon opened her mouth.

An avalanche of molten fire roared towards the Lords. They crouched, clenching their fists and a protective bubble appeared around them. The flames slid off and poured down the wall. Toth-Haden took another huge gulp and breathed again. This time the conflagration hit the structure full on.

"Oh my God," Charlie croaked from the carrier. "It's melting."

Slowly, the Great Wall caught fire and began to dissolve, collapsing in on itself. The wizards vanished, screaming, into a molten crevasse. Toth-Haden rose in a leisurely arc, one rolling eye turning to the Galhadrian troops. The Rath leapt up and down, gurgling and spitting with glee.

"I fear it is our turn," Ganieda balled her fists and raised both arms, determined to go down fighting.

Two white plumes shot into the air, twisting and turning, hitting Toth-Haden in her underbelly. There was a huge explosion and the dragon roared in agony, sending a spout of fire into the air. Before she could recover, another pair of vapour trails raced into the sky. They arched at the last moment and vanished into the beast's maw.

There was a muffled rumble, and the creature's throat exploded, bone and guts raining over the landscape. Toth-Haden plunged down, crashing into the remains of the Great Wall and demolishing the structure completely.

''Heat-seeking missiles." A cover slid open on the front of the armoured carrier and Peazle's eyes appeared in the slit. "Like I kept telling Jack Thane, humans have a completely different kind of magic."

The jeers and laughter of the Rath had turned to horrified silence.

"The enemy are confused and demoralised." Arthur raised his arm again. "This is the moment to strike."

He spurred his mount into a gallop.

"Chaaaaaarge!"

500 horses thundered across the plain towards the Rath, Galhadrian forces running behind, screaming defiance. The front ranks of the enemy tried to retreat but had nowhere to go. Then Morgana was among them, cursing and spitting, urging her followers forward. The Rath broke into a shambling lope.

The gap between the forces narrowed. 1,000 yards. Then 500. Then 200.

Arthurs knights suddenly halted. The centre four moved aside and, into the gap, rumbled the armoured car, driven by Inspector Archer.

Two more missiles sped into the Rath's massed ranks, blowing upon an enormous hole. The 30 mm cannon and coaxial machine gun opened fire. On top of the turret, Charlie let loose with the second machine gun, sweeping it in wide arcs. Spent casings bounced and pinged around him.

"Say hello to my leetle friend!" he crowed. "Saw that in a movie once."

The first 20 or 30 lines of the Rath were annihilated. The rest tried to surge forward, using sheer weight of numbers to reach their foe. It did no good.

Rank after rank went down as they floundered against a wall of bullets and artillery shells. Morgana let out a cry of rage, pushed her way back into the throng and disappeared. She knew, only too well, that she was not impervious to silver bullets.

With a wail, the Rath turned and ran, leaving thousands of bodies behind.

"That went well." Peazle jumped down from the vehicle and saluted Arthur. "We've got them on the run."

"We've simply made them more cautious," his king replied. "I imagine the next attack will come after dark."

"That is perfectly fine by me," the boy smiled. "This thing has night scopes and headlights."

# Night Falls

"Morgana has great influence over dark creatures," Gorrodin said. "But she must have truly formidable powers to be able to wake and command a dragon."

"Got any good news?" Charlie asked.

"Toth-Haden must have been the last of her race. If not, another would be among us by now."

"Thank heavens for small mercies."

The Clan were gathered in a hastily erected tent. The rest of the army had built small fires and were resting. Some were roasting dragon meat, renowned for giving strength and vitality to those who ate it.

Duncan sorely wanted to go and see his brother, but this was a war council and he felt he should be part of it.

"How are you for ammunition?" he asked Peazle.

"Four missiles left. Enough shells and bullets to pull off the same trick one more time. Then we will be out."

He pulled a silver handgun from his pocket.

"The small arms haven't been touched yet. We'll use them once the armoured car's weapons are spent."

"The Rath favour the dark and Morgana won't be fooled twice," Gorrodin said. "If we can hold off a night attack, we will stand a better chance the following day."

"That's a big if." Duncan looked up to where the sun had almost sunk below the hills. "If we're gonnae come up wi a plan, we'd better do it fast."

"What about launching a sneaky attack ourselves?" Shadowjack asked. "Morgana won't expect that."

"With good reason," the wizard snorted. "Further back, where the plain narrows, the mountains are riddled with caves. And no doubt, they are filled with Rath. If we ventured too far, they would pour down and surround us. We have no choice but to wait for them to come at us once night falls."

"You and I can light up the sky," Ganieda said. "Make them a better target."

"That would help," her brother conceded. "But use up most of our strength. We'd be useless in battle."

"It is far from ideal." Arthur was hunched over a table, looking at a map of the area. "But we have little choice. Archer?"

"Yes, sir?"

"When they charge, use up the rest of your ammunition, then retreat immediately."

"Understood."

"Galhadrians have sharper eyes than humans. I will station them along the foot of the mountains, for the Rath will try to sneak along that way, sticking to the shadows. My knights will stay behind the armoured carrier, ready to take over, once it leaves."

He turned to Archer.

"You *will* leave on my order. You have my son and Gorrodin's daughter with you."

"Not going to attempt any heroics, don't worry."

"Then let's get a couple of hours rest."

"May I go see my brother, Sire?" Duncan leapt to his feet.

"Of course." Arthur went back to his map. Charlie tapped him on the shoulder and the man looked round.

"Sorry, boy. I've been a bit preoccupied." He embraced his son. "I want to say how proud I am of the way you've acted."

"Thanks, dad. Now how about making *me* proud?"

"What do you mean?"

"I mean, you saunter into battle without flinching, but you're scared of talking to your own wife."

"Too right, I am."

"Do it for me." Charlie took his dad's hand and led him over to his mum. Ganieda was seated in a corner of the tent, a picture of misery.

"We have been together forever, it seems." Arthur knelt beside her. "And never disagreed before."

"This is more than a disagreement." The woman's face was pinched with fury. "I tried to protect my boy. You put him in the middle of a battlefield."

"Right," Charlie snapped. "Stop using me as an excuse, you two."

His parents' eyes widened.

"You are each other's worlds," the boy continued. "Sure, you love me, but not as much as each other, and I have no problem with that. In fact, I think it's rather wonderful."

His parents began to object, but Charlie cut them off.

"Mother? You did what you thought was right, despite the cost. Father? You did what *you* thought was right too. Your aims were at odds, but neither of you were wrong. So let's cut to the chase."

A frown clouded his brow.

"How dare you both deny me the opportunity to do the same? I am the son of a Lord of the Western Wilderness and the fabled King Arthur. I have fought the Rath and won. I hold the Great Sword. Quite frankly, I expect to be treated as an equal and it disappoints me greatly that you do not."

"Told you he was picking up our way of talking," Arthur winced.

"So move on and stop acting like teenagers in a playground spat." Charlie wagged a finger at them. "Bloody well kiss and make up."

Arthur and Ganieda looked into each other's eyes. Finally, they both smiled. Charlie was right. They had been in love for centuries, and nothing could change that.

"My king." Ganieda stood and opened her arms. Arthur sank gratefully into them. He motioned for Charlie and the boy joined their embrace.

Gorrodin looked around. Lilly was standing a few feet away.

"Come, daughter." He held out his hand. "Let us walk and talk, as we used to, long ago. I would hear of your adventures."

"You read my mind back at the falls," Lilly said shyly.

"A poor substitute for hearing them from your own lips. My heart is sore at the years I have missed and how little time we have to be together."

Lilly took his arm and they strolled across the darkening plain.

Duncan found his brother seated beside a campfire with his mount.

"So, what dae I call you?" he asked. "Caleb or Galahad?"

"I am Galahad to everyone here," the man replied. "But I know it is a name borrowed from another, long dead, warrior. To you, I am Caleb, and that is good enough for me."

Beside them, his horse nibbled at the grass.

Now that Duncan's great quest was at an end, he wasn't sure how to proceed.

"I'm not much of a talker," he admitted. "I dinnae rightly ken what tae say."

"I do not see that we stand much chance in the coming fight." Caleb patted his steed's nose. "Therefore, I am grateful for your company, even if you stay silent."

"No. You are my only kin and I cannae hold my tongue, even if you may not want tae hear what I have to say."

And he told Caleb everything, including what he knew of the Dolorous Stroke.

When he was finished, the man sat quietly for a long time.

"If you were tae ride away now, I would understand," Duncan said.

"I will not desert my comrades nor abandon my brother," Caleb replied. "But there is one more story I would like to hear."

"Anything."

The knight moved closer until his shoulder was touching Duncan's.

"Tell me about our father and mother."

# The Sky Aflame

There was a commotion outside the tent and Peazle burst in.

"Two people seek an audience, my lady," he said. "Demand it, in fact."

Ganieda let go of her family.

"Who is it," she asked. "I am rather preoccupied."

"Oh, I think you'll recognise them."

The tent flap opened and a pair of figures pushed their way through. Ganieda exhaled loudly and Arthur's hand went to his sword hilt.

"Yes. It takes more than a damned dragon to kill us."

Jack Thane and Math stood before them, clothes tattered and torn. Their gashed faces were caked with blood, and Thane leaned heavily on an ash staff. One of Math's arms hung limply by her side.

"Where are the other Lords?" Arthur rose to his feet.

"Dead." There was no emotion in the wizard's voice. "And we are grievously hurt, as you can see."

"I will heal your wounds as best I can." Gorrodin and Lilly entered behind them. "Stay still."

"Do not waste your magic, old man." Math waved him away. "The Rath are massing as we speak."

"I will muster the men." Arthur got to his feet. "My love? You and Gorrodin must light up the sky, as we discussed. Lady Math and Lord Thane? I beg you to assist them."

"That is a poor plan," Thane sniffed. "We cannot match the sun and, despite our best efforts, many deep shadows will remain for those creatures to hide in."

"It's the only move open to us," Artur retorted. "Unless you have a better idea."

"I always do." Thane cast a glance at Math and she nodded.

"I know you think me a monster," he continued. "But I swore an oath to do my utmost for Galhadria and my resolution has always been firm. I would have ruled in the same way."

He stood as erect as he could manage.

"You may have despised my methods, but times change. I merely reflected that." He turned to Ganieda. "I wished to kill two birds with one stone, as humans say."

Charlie's mother could not meet his gaze.

"Humanity is as great a threat to us as the Rath, and I feel you know that in your heart. One day, I will be proved right."

"You were talking about a plan?" Arthur was un-moved.

"Save your troops until morning, when they stand a chance, no matter how slim. Math and I shall hold Morgana at bay until daylight."

"That is suicide." Gorrodin shook his head. "I will not hear of it."

"With Tom Lincoln gone," Thane snapped. "I lead the Lords, or what is left of them. I am not asking for permission."

He gave a thin smile.

"I used to love travelling this land, singing ballads," he said. "It would have been nice to hear one was written about how I met my fate. Just a shame there will be nobody left to recount it."

"And you, Math?"

"I cannot sing a note." The woman kept her face straight. "I will go with Master Thane. He would have made a great leader, you know. Though, it seemed only I could see it."

"I'm beginning to get an inking." Gorrodin stared at Thane. "You still could be, for we are not dead yet. You could both transport yourself somewhere else."

"As could you."

"My place is here, I am afraid."

"Mine too. A ruler with no kingdom will never recover from the pain of its loss." Thane winked at Arthur. "Isn't that right, my Lord?"

It was Arthur's turn to look away.

Charlie watched his dad's reaction. Here was a man who had gone from being the saviour of a nation to a circus acrobat, entertaining small crowds. That must have hurt deep inside.

"Once, we were good friends." Gorrodin shook Thane's hand. "I consider us to be so again."

"I suppose so. Pity you are rotten at playing the lute."

Thane and Math put up their hoods and left without a backwards glance. The Clan trooped out and watched the pair limp across the plain, until darkness swallowed them.

Duncan and Caleb piled more hastily gathered wood on the fire. In the distance, they could hear the growls and grunts as the Rath gathered.

"Why have no orders come from our king?" Caleb looked pensive. "We should be on our horses and ready to repel the enemy."

"I dinnae ken." Duncan was equally puzzled. "But I swear I saw two figures heading towards them."

"It cannot be an attempt to parlay." Caleb stroked his nervous steed. "After what you told me, we know Morgana will settle for nothing but total victory."

A flash lit the night and the brothers jumped. The nearest horses backed away, snorting in panic and the other knights clasped their muzzles, calming them.

A sea of flame leapt up in the distance and they could suddenly see ranks of creatures writhing and burning. In the centre of the conflagration were Jack Thane and Math, laying waste to the foe. Bolts of lightning shot from their fingers, lancing through the enemy.

As the beasts shrank back, Thane and Math staggered forwards, pushing into the screaming mass. Soon they were encircled and hidden from sight, still emanating death and destruction.

"I have seen many acts of bravery in my time," Caleb lamented. "But none like this."

"Whoever they are, they met their death tae give us a chance,"

Duncan unsheathed his sword and held it up. One by one, the 500 knights did the same, the reflections of firelight mingling with the far off inferno, flickering along the blades.

Jack Thane and Math were almost spent. The Rath were warily closing in around them.

"It is time." Thane pulled his talisman from inside the folds of his cloak. His companion did the same.

"Mistress Math? It has been one of the great privileges of..."

"Oh, shut up." The woman grabbed Thane's head and kissed him on the lips. "You and I need no words."

She stepped back and smiled.

"Been wanting to do that for a century or more."

Seeing their chance, the Rath charged. As their claws ripped into them, Jack Thane and Math smashed the talismans together.

The explosion lit up the plain with the force of a dozen suns, a dazzling lethal luminescence that spread for half a mile. It annihilated thousands of Morgana's forces, scorching grass and sending rocks tumbling down the mountain screes, burying hundreds more creatures inside their caves.

As the darkness descended again, the Rath retreated once more, until the valley was silent - save for the cheering of Arthur's men.

The Clan watched the deaths of Jack Thane and Math with open mouths.

"Surely they'll give up," Inspector Archer ventured. "Morgana must have lost more than half her force by now."

"She cares not for casualties," Arthur corrected. "Not when she is guaranteed victory."

He motioned for the rest of them to follow.

"Into the tent," he commanded. "Peazle? Fetch Duncan and his brother. I have a story to tell you."

# Daybreak

The Clan waited until Duncan and Caleb joined them. They sat down, all except Arthur.

"When I was king," he began. "The round table and I fought the Rath, as most of you know. They lost and we won but it was a pyrrhic victory."

"What's that then?" Shadowjack asked. "I get enough big words thrown at me from Peazle."

"It's a victory that inflicts such a devastating toll on the winner, it negates any true sense of achievement." Peazle was always quick to show off his knowledge.

"Aye. That doesn't help. I don't know what negate means either."

"It means the king won, but his men were almost wiped out in the process."

"Indeed." Arthur nodded. "The Rath's reign of terror was ended, yet the toll on us was immense. Only four of my knights were left alive. I was mortally wounded and the round table destroyed. Without us, the country slipped back into lawlessness."

"I see what you are getting at," Gorrodin nodded. "We must do to the Rath what they once did to us."

"They are destined to win," Arthur agreed. "But what if we take almost all of them with us? Say we managed to kill all but a handful?"

"They would be still the victors," Duncan said. "But without the numbers tae do any further damage."

"They will simply breed again," Ganieda pointed out. "Or infect others left in Galhadria."

"Then we must act quickly." Arthur motioned for Duncan's brother to rise.

"You must ride back across the land. Tell the remaining inhabitants to seek refuge in Alabarra, The Wooded Kingdom and Monshorn."

"They aren't exactly friends of ours," Peazle reminded him. "They consider the Little People to be arrogant and insular."

"They are not exactly enemies either," Caleb argued. "For I have travelled their lands and rid them of many a monster."

"They are not warlike and have sat on the fence so far," Duncan added. "But news travels fast, and they will soon ken what the Rath are capable of, if they dinnae already."

"Then urge them to raise a force quickly and ride into Galhadria," Arthur said. "Wipe out the few creatures we could not defeat before the Rath gain a foothold and come for *them*."

"Tell them they *can* secure victory." Charlie snapped his fingers. "For none of those kingdoms were involved in the Dolorous Stroke."

"Precisely," Arthur smiled solemnly. "This army will not live to see it, but Galhadria will be saved."

"I should have trusted you." Ganieda beamed. "Charlie and Lilly can accompany him. All the kids can."

"I do not wish to seem ungrateful, My Lord," Caleb said. "But my place is by my brother's side."

"Of course it is. So the rest of the Clan will go with you. I trust only the best."

A silence descended as each member considered this. One last chance to avoid certain death.

"I can't." Charlie was the first to speak. "I am the guardian of Excalibur."

"The Great Sword is rightfully mine, boy."

"Not anymore. It has chosen me." Charlie refused to back down. "Besides, how would it look if the king's own son fled and left his forces to their fate."

"Oh, please, no." Ganieda pleaded.

"Those Luddites you command don't have a clue how to operate an armoured car or work a machine gun." Peazle fastened his waistcoat. "I'm staying."

"I'm the designated driver," Inspector Archer rubbed his bald head. "Been in many a high-speed chase, too."

"I man the cannons," Lilly cracked her knuckles.

"We're not leaving our pals," Shadowjack and Duncan shook their heads.

"This is the wish of your commander!" Arthur pulled himself up to his full height. "You will do as I say!"

"You're my father, not my commander," Charlie retorted. "In fact, none of the Clan are actually in your army."

Arthur's shoulders slumped.

"What if I said please?"

"Sorry, dad. My mind is made up. I'm not deserting you and mum."

"I *am* bound by your orders, Sire." Caleb got to his feet. "Though I beg you to reconsider."

"As you said, you have travelled the lands of Alabarra, The Wooded Kingdom and Monshorn. If the Clan will not go, take the three Galhadrians with the fastest steeds instead."

"As you wish." Caleb cast a lost look at Duncan. "I am truly sorry, brother."

"I'm not, for at least you will be safe."

Caleb saluted Arthur, lips tight, and pushed his way out of the tent.

"I don't suppose you and Gorrodin would consider accompanying him?" Arthur knelt down by Ganieda. "Galhadria will need new Lords to rule in the unstable times coming."

"And leave you and Charlie. Not a chance."

"We can wreak more havoc on the Rath than all your knights combined." Gorrodin put his arm around Lilly. "So, no."

"Not much bloody use being king if nobody does what I say," Arthur grumped, sounding remarkably like his old self.

"Pull yourself together, dad." Charlie pinched his father's cheek with false bravado. "You have a pyrrhic defeat to engineer. So get thinking. It's daybreak."

The Clan trooped out of the tent, leaving Arthur and Ganieda alone.

"I tried, dear." The man sank to the ground beside his wife. "I really did."

"I know." Ganieda kissed his weary forehead. "Our son is as stubborn as us, and I love him all the more for it."

"I must lead from the front, as I always have." Arthur spread out a map of the valley on the ground. "You stay by Charlie as much as you are able. Protect him to the end."

"Of course." His wife shook her head miserably. "We've been terrible parents, haven't we?"

"Absolutely." But Arthur couldn't keep the pride from his voice. "Yet what an incredible son we managed to raise."

The king rode to the front of his army. He was resplendent in silver armour, a plume of red spouting from his helmet. On the other side of the plain, the Rath were gathering once more.

There was no sign of Morgana. He assumed she was wisely staying at the back. She was powerful but not indestructible.

"We are still vastly outnumbered, as you can plainly see." Arthur began. "But why would we want more soldiers?"

Sitting on top of the armoured carrier, Charlie frowned. This seemed an odd way for the king to raise his troop's spirits.

"If we are going to die, the less of us, the better, is that not so? But the fewer the men, the greater share of honour."

Arthur lowered his voice, though the troops could still hear him perfectly.

"Still, if any of you want to leave, you are free to do so."

This time, Charlie groaned out loud. What was his dad up to? Many of his troops certainly looked tempted by the offer. But Arthur wasn't finished.

"Think about this, though," he yelled. "Our battle shall go down in history. It will be remembered forever, in legend, and so will you, just for being here."

He stood up in the saddle.

"Your descendants will sing songs and tell stories of how we few, we happy few, became a band of brothers. For anyone who fights with me today *is* my brother!"

A whoop rose from the ranks.

"When other Galhadrians try to boast of the great things they have achieved," Arthur continued at the top of his lungs. "Your children can make them fall silent and bow their heads by simply saying these words."

He raised a gleaming sword in the air.

"I fought alongside my king against the Rath!"

The army roared and stamped their feet. Charlie gave his father a thumbs up.

Standing next to him, Ganieda raised a shapely eyebrow.

"Yes, yes." Arthur winked at her. "I knicked most of that speech from William Shakespeare."

He slammed down his visor.

"Let us commence battle."

# Lancelot

The Galhadrian army took the same formation as they had the day before.

In the vanguard were the 500 knights, with the armoured carrier at its centre. Behind that were Ganieda and Gorrodin, flanked by Duncan and Shadowjack, who had abandoned their unfamiliar mounts and were now on foot. To the rear were the Galhadrian troops.

Arthur sat astride his steed, a few yards in front of his army, horribly exposed. Yet, he seemed to show no fear. Once again, Charlie marvelled at the change in his meek and mild father. He was beginning to see that a true leader could wear many faces.

Opposite them, the Rath sensed triumph and Morgana was encouraging them from the safety of the back. This time the creatures were determined not to run, no matter how high the casualties.

Which was exactly what Arthur hoped and feared in equal measure.

His men knew what to do. Gorrodin had spirited the plan into their minds, using magic, in case Morgana had spies watching. It had used up precious power, but it meant she had no inkling of their strategy.

In essence, however, the idea was simplicity itself. Kill as many of the enemy as possible before they were overwhelmed.

The Rath whooped and screeched, making little runs and then retreating, trying to unnerve their foe. Arthur knew any delay would only weaken the morale of his troops.

"I am the knight with 1,000 eyes." He shouted across the valley. "And I see your doom!"

He charged towards the enemy and the 500 galloped after him. Archer revved the armoured car into life and the Galhadrians followed, roaring a battle cry.

With blood-curdling screeches, the Rath scampered out to meet them, bristling with claws and teeth.

Arthur veered left and, once again, the knights split in two, heading for the enemy flanks as close to the steeply rising cliffs as they could manage, leaving the armoured vehicle in the centre.

Morgana's forces were not going to be fooled twice. They parted and surged towards the mountains to meet the knights, leaving as few in the middle as they could, waiting to be annihilated by machine gun fire.

The last two rockets streamed from the armoured car. But they were not aimed at the Rath.

The creatures looked up, astonished, as the white plumes soared high over their heads and kept going. Near the end of the valley, the missiles crashed into the sheer cliff faces and exploded three-quarters of the way up.

As the sonic boom faded, it was replaced by a sound like nails being dragged across a blackboard, and rocks cascaded down onto the Rath. Then both cliff faces sagged and collapsed, burying hundreds of the streaming creatures under tons of falling rubble. Huge boulders filled the valley floor, effectively cutting Morgana's forces in half.

The armoured car shot forward through the gap in the middle of the Rath's forces, spitting lead in all directions. Its cannons roared, and more of the cliff face peeled off and fell. The knights wheeled around and headed back the way they had come, while the Galhadrians crashed into the Rath, sweeping them away.

As the enemy centre collapsed, the flanks tried to circle the gap and trap the Galhadrians. Instead, they ran into a hail of machine gun fire. Then the knights wheeled again and joined the fray, slamming into the creatures from either side.

The rear half of Morgana's army began scrabbling over the barrier of rubble, but the guns switched and raked the top. The front half of the Rath tried to retreat but found themselves trapped between Arthur's troops and the wall of boulders. By the time the guns ran out of ammo, it was too late.

Within ten minutes, it was over. Not a monster was left alive.

Arthur spun his hand. His army turned and headed back to the remains of the Great Wall.

There they regrouped and waited.

The Clan whispered to each other, casting glances at Arthur, who sat calmly on his charger. Finally, Duncan strode over, with the rest bunched behind him.

"Your plan worked perfectly, my Lord." He bowed. "But we dinnae understand why ye retreated."

He indicated the barrier of slabs and boulders between them and the rest of Morgana's forces.

"Thon beasties will have to climb up that and doon the other side tae engage us. We could easily pick them off, as they do so."

"True," Arthur said. "And Morgana knows that, as well. There is no rule to say she has to win this battle today. If we stayed, she would wait for nightfall again, then begin removing the rocks under cover of darkness."

"So we're just going tae let her entire army climb over and get intae formation, withoot doing anything?"

"Correct." Arthur smiled. "I used the same trick when I first encountered the Rath. They will only attack if they are confident of success. If we are lucky, they will think we retreated because the armoured car ran out of bullets."

"Well... it has."

"So they will commit everything to one last foray. They do not know Ganieda and Gorrodin are with us and, this time, they will have a wall of rocks at their backs."

"So they cannae retreat."

"Nor can we." Arthur dismounted. "This is the end game, my young friend. Take the opportunity to rest. The enemy does not have that luxury."

"I will not have another chance tae say it." Duncan saluted. "But thank you for saving my brother."

"You are most welcome."

Arthur's army sat and talked nervously, watching the Rath climb over the rubble and slowly gather on the plain.

"There's a lot less of them than before," Shadow-jack Henry peered over his shoulder every few minutes. "But they still outnumber us five to one."

"All the more tae kill," Duncan grunted.

"You're a bloodthirsty wee devil, aren't you?"

Arthur was moving through his army, praising and thanking them. Charlie sidled up to his mother.

"Still mad at me, my lady?"

"Oh, God. Just call me mum." The woman embraced him. "I am still mad at you but also incredibly honoured that you are mine."

She pointed to Peazle, Duncan and Lilly.

"They look like youths but have lived a long, long time. What would make a boy like you sacrifice himself when you have your whole life ahead?"

"Galhadria is full of children, with their whole lives ahead. I'm just one person, and this is where I am needed."

He rested his head on his mother's shoulder.

"I don't mind admitting I'm terrified, though."

"It's not too late for…"

"I told you," Charlie interrupted. "I'm staying."

He paused.

"And maybe I'm hoping for a miracle. How come I don't have any magical powers? I'm half Galhadrian, after all."

"I'm afraid you take after your father. Human. A dreamer. Someone who cannot bear to see wrongs without trying to right them."

She pulled him tighter.

"And the noblest man who ever lived."

"I guess that will have to do."


The Rath were almost ready, a few final stragglers lurching over the wall. In the far distance, they could see Morgana, a tiny figure hurrying them along.

The Clan gathered for a final farewell. They shook hands and hugged but were mostly silent. Then they sat in a ring, lost in their own thoughts.

"If you don't mind, I'd like to say a few words." Inspector Archer got to his feet. The rest stared at him in surprise. He was normally so quiet it was easy to forget he was there.

"Go ahead, my friend." Arthur motioned for him to continue.

"I'm a true outsider here," he said. "None of you even know my first name. And so, I look at you all from that perspective. Earlier I watched you debate who to save, Galhadria or humanity."

"It was no easy decision…" Gorrodin began.

"No," Arthur commanded. "Let him say his piece."

Archer cleared his throat.

"I'm a policeman," he said. "That in itself means nothing. There are good and bad cops. But it doesn't alter what we're supposed to do. Protect innocents from those who'd prey on them."

He brought out his badge.

"Right and wrong are complex concepts and painful to uphold - yet underneath is something very simple. Help others. Don't put yourself and your desires first."

He glanced around.

"Here I see humans, Galhadrians and those in between, held by a bond. Friendship. You talk of losing, but that's also a concept. We'll be wiped out, yes. But we won't have lost. Our names may vanish. But what we did will live on."

He dropped the badge into the mud and sat down.

"I don't need a symbol to remind me of what I do. I fight monsters."

There was a stunned silence.

"What *is* your first name?" Peazle asked quietly.

"Walter."

"Not anymore." Arthur stood and drew his sword. "If you would do me the honour?"

He placed the blade on Inspector Archer's shoulder.

"Of all my lost knights, there was one I favoured above all others. He was humble, brave and principled beyond all calling. You remind me of him."

He raised the weapon and placed it on the other shoulder.

"From now on, you will be known as Sir Lancelot Du Lac, Knight of Joyous Gard."

# The Final Battle

The opposing forces faced each other for the last time. Once more, Gorrodin sent out a subliminal message to Arthur's force, conveying his new strategy. It was a simple enough message. Fight to the last man.

Then the king rode to the front of his army.

"I have no great speech to give this time," he cried. "We have reduced the Rath from one hundred thousand to ten thousand. Now, all we can do is buy time for our families."

He lifted his sword.

"Are you ready?"

The din of swords rattling on shields was deafening.

"Bowmen, let loose!"

All Galhadrians knew archery. But Gorrodin had used magic to transform their simple hunting weapons into longbows. Arthur knew how powerful a firearm they could be. He had fought at the Battle of Agincourt.

The sky turned dark with arrows. They fell among the Rath like black rain, decimating them. Before the monsters could recover and other deadly hail sailed into the air and landed among them.

The beasts charged.

Arthur's archers had time for one more volley. Then they dropped the bows and picked up their swords and shields.

This time, the knights stayed where they were and half the Galhadrian force charged instead, two tightly packed ranks stretching across the valley floor. The enemies raced towards each other screaming war cries.

Twenty yards from their foe, the Galhadrians skidded to a halt. Each man locked eyes with the creature heading toward him, as if daring it to come on. The mass of Rath showed no hesitation, eager to break this thin line of resistance. They were so focused, they did not notice the 500 knights gathering in a V formation, like the point of a spear, with Arthur at the front. Did not see them break into a gallop.

As they reached their prey, each Galhadrian thrust his sword forwards. But not at the creature they had been watching so carefully. Instead, every thrust was aimed at the monster to the right of them. It was a blind blow but could not fail to connect with such a tightly packed group.

The entire front line of the Rath fell.

The Galhadrian vanguard turned and fled, leaving the next line exposed. But they did not attempt to fight, for their swords were still sheathed. Each man threw a spear at the second rank of the enemy. Another swathe of the creatures collapsed, clutching impaled throats and chests.

The second row of Galhadrians spun and retreated as quickly as they could run.

The creatures attempted to catch them but had to scramble over the bodies of their fallen comrades, stumbling and sliding in pools of blood. By the time they had done so, The Galhadrians were twenty yards ahead.

The Rath gibbered and jeered. The enemy was fast but they knew they could outpace them. Besides, the Galhadrians were heading right for the hurtling knights, and the two groups would surely collide in a tangled mess of armour and bodies. Victory was theirs at last!

The Galhadrians suddenly dropped to the ground and rolled onto their backs, shields braced across their torsos. The 500 hundred knights dug in their spurs, and the horses leapt over the prone bodies of their comrades.

In a flash, the Galhadrians were on their once more, joining the rest of their force sprinting behind the 500.

A forest of lances impaled the Rath and were quickly released as armoured warhorses slammed into the enemy. The knights drew their swords and began to hack and slash. The V widened, forcing the creatures apart and the armoured car surged into the gap, crushing beasts under its tracks. It was followed by the entire Galhadrian army.

Now it was every man for themselves.

Arthur was an unstoppable force, slicing and cutting in all directions. The Galhadrians fought with the fury that only those defending their homeland can muster. Gorrodin and Ganieda leapt down from the rear of the armoured vehicle, bolts of lightning shooting from their fingers, burning smouldering paths through the shrieking monsters.

But the numbers they were facing were insurmountable. Rath surrounded the armoured car and swarmed over the top, trying to prise open the hatches. Others began to rock the vehicle from side to side. Ganieda and Gorrodin did their best to destroy them but were pushed further and further away, forced to defend themselves, rather than protecting their children.

With a screech of tortured metal, the armoured car toppled over. The turret hatch opened and the Rath whooped in triumph, ready to worm their way inside.

They were met with a hail of silver bullets. Charlie and Peazle crawled out, firing as they went, followed by Lilly and Inspector Archer. Charlie and Archer held Thompson M192 Machine Guns, while Peazle had an Uzi in each hand. They got to their feet and advanced, spraying death in all directions.

Lilly didn't need a weapon. Though her powers could not match that of Gorrodin or Ganieda, she was perfectly capable of defending herself. She thrust out both hands and a dozen snarling creatures dissolved in front of her.

Flashes of light showed where Ganieda and her brother were holding back the foe. Arthur was nowhere in sight. Charlie spotted Shadowjack and Duncan to their right. Duncan was whirling like a dervish, his sword a blur, while Shadowjack swung his black-smith's hammer, breaking heads as if they were eggs.

Incredible as it seemed, Arthur's army was holding its own.

Morgana finally appeared.

She headed for Gorrodin first, sweeping men and horses from her path. The wizard understood her intentions immediately. She was coming after his talisman.

"Hold her back," he hissed to Ganieda, for he knew his powers were useless against his former wife. Once again, he cursed himself for sharing the Grail with her.

Ganieda rubbed her hands together and sent a blast of light pulsing towards Morgana. It lifted her into the air and sent the creature flying back several yards.

But Morgana had grown too strong. Within seconds, she was on her feet and lurching forwards.

Gorrodin threw the cup in the air and batted it, as if he were playing tennis. It sailed over the heads of the battling throng and found its way to Lilly. She plucked it from the sky and hid it in the folds of her cloak.

With a scream of fury, Morgana changed direction and headed towards her daughter.

The Clan had formed a tight circle, back to back, with Lilly in the centre. They struck, parried and fired, enveloped in a haze of oily smoke and spattering blood.

Morgana was cutting her way through Arthur's forces as if they were flies to be swatted. At the sight of her, the Rath were invigorated, doubling their efforts.

"Concentrate your fire on Morgana," Charlie shouted. "Cut her down!"

Her minions leapt in the way, hiding their leader as she dodged and weaved, using her forces as inhuman shields. This gruesome game of hide and seek continued until Charlie, Archer and Peazle finally ran out of bullets.

Morgana rushed forwards and batted Archer's gun from his hands, raking her claws across his chest. The man groaned and sank to his knees in the mud. Morgana leapt away from the swords, grinning maniacally.

"Save yourselves," Duncan commanded. "We'll deal wi this horror."

He and Shadowjack advanced.

From the corner of his eye, Charlie saw Peazle dart back to the armoured car, worm his way inside and shut the hatch. Charlie couldn't blame him. The boy wasn't a fighter and no longer had a weapon.

Shadowjack swung his hammer but Morgana ducked, sank her talons into his side and flung the giant away, knocking over assailants as if they were ninepins. Duncan moved forwards, trying to reach her, but this determination was his undoing. He went down, four of the Rath clinging to him like leeches.

"Run, Lilly," Charlie hissed. "You can't let Morgana get hold of the Grail, or we'll be finished in minutes."

"Don't you dare die," Lilly blasted open a path and fled through the hole she had made in the enemy ranks. Charlie dropped his empty gun and pulled out Excalibur. At the sight of the Great Sword, the Rath shrank back, snarling and making tentative lunges at the boy. A few lopped off arms had them retreating again.

Their leader showed no such hesitation, taking off after Lilly. Her soldiers parted to allow faster passage.

"Hey, ugly!" Charlie yelled. "I'm the one who killed your son! You going to let that go unavenged?"

Morgana stopped in her tracks. Tiny malevolent eyes fastened on the boy and a chill ran up his spine. But he had to give Lilly a chance.

"That's right!" he shouted. "The big bully cried for his mum as he died."

Morgana started towards him, claws twitching. Then, for the first time, she spoke.

"When I am finished, I ssswear will make you do the ssssame."

"Got the same stupid lisp as Mordred, eh?" Charlie grinned. "Must run in the family."

Morgana drew in a deep breath and ground two rows of vicious teeth, trying to control her anger.

"He isssss not to be harmed," she rasped to her underlings. "I will return and make him beg for death myssself."

Then she chased after Lilly.

"Damn!" Charlie raced to cut her off. To his astonishment, the Rath refusing to touch him.

"At least being on Morgana's bad side makes it easier to get around."

He found Lilly, trapped in a ring of snarling creatures. Her magic was at an end, weak sparks emanating from her fingers. The Rath parted to let Morgana through and she advanced on the girl.

"The cup isssss mine," she gurgled. "Give it to me."

Lilly pulled the Grail from inside her cloak. For a second, she considered handing it over. Yet, she knew Morgana would not spare her. In desperation, she looked for someone to throw it to.

"Not yet, Toothy Mctoothface." Charlie appeared between Morgana and her daughter. "In a long line of mistakes, you just made another."

He held Excalibur out.

"Want to try your luck against the Great Sword?"

"You are indeed a worthy adversssary." Morgana sounded surprised. "I have underessstimated you, as my sssson did."

"It's no use, Charlie," Lilly sobbed. "I have no talisman of my own. And you have no magic."

Then it struck the boy. A simple, obvious fact. He recalled Jack Thane's words from long ago.

*You have formed a bond with the weapon for reasons I do not comprehend. It has chosen you.*

"I may not have magic, but I *do* have a talisman," he cried. "And I share it with you."

He handed the Great Sword to Lilly.

"Now, get us the hell out of here."

The girl tapped Excalibur against the cup and muttered an incantation. A blue, glowing portal opened behind her and Morgana gaped.

"Kill them both!" she screamed.

Lilly and Charlie leapt into the light. Morgana scooped up an axe and threw it after them. Then she dived through the closing aperture.

The light faded and the creatures milled around in confusion.

Charlie, Lilly and Morgana were gone.

# The Whistle

Charlie sprawled, headfirst, in long, lush grass, then jumped to his feet. Excalibur was sticking out of the damp soil. He grabbed the hilt in time to see Morgana emerge from the closing portal. There was no sign of Lilly or the Grail.

"Looks like it's you and me again," He pointed the sword at her. "Another stalemate, eh?"

"Sssso it would sssseem." To his astonishment, Morgana smiled, revealing two rows of jagged teeth. "I fear the Great Sword but I do not tire, like you. I will wait for night to fall and then you will be mine."

"I seem to remember Mordred saying much the same thing. But I'm still here."

"Taunting me will make revenge all the sssweeter. In the meantime I ssshall hunt for the cup."

Her grin faded as she looked past the boy.

"Where are we?"

Charlie risked a glance over his shoulder. The mountain of Leiter Dhuibh soared upwards and Eas a Chual Aluinn Falls sparkled as it cascaded down one side.

"You don't recognise it?" He masked his own astonishment. "The Grail has taken Lilly to the last place and time she was truly happy."

"It cannot be." Morgana's tiny eyes registered shock. On the other side of a wide swathe of pastureland, dotted with wildflowers, was a stone cottage. Smoke rose from the chimney, and a few chickens pecked and scuffed around the front door.

It was her daughter's home. *Her* home. Confusion flickered over the creature's face.

"I do not wisssh to be here."

"Neither do I," Charlie admitted. "I think I know what happens next and it's not something I ever wanted to experience again."

"What do you mean?" Morgana tapped her head with a yellow claw. "It is ssso long ago that I cannot remember."

"In that case, you're in for a hell of a shock."


Lilly appeared in the meadow, playing with a dog. She did not resemble the tired and bloodstained girl Morgana had chased through the portal. This was a younger version, happy and carefree, singing a song and picking daisies.

They heard a rumble in the distance that transformed quickly into the thunder of horse's hooves.

Morgana emerged from the house, into the sunlight. Not the abomination she would become, but a beautiful woman in a velvet dress. Her hands shot to her mouth as she spotted whooping horsemen galloping across the moor towards her daughter. Their faces were daubed with blue and all were heavily armed. Their savage cries sounded remarkably like those of the Rath.

"Picts!" She breathed. "A war party!"

Lilly had spotted the horsemen and was sprinting back towards the safety of the house - but it was obvious the Picts would catch her before she reached shelter. Morgana was about to head for her daughter then, realizing the same thing, turned and darted back indoors.

Lilly was still racing for safety. Her dog turned and bounded towards the attackers in a desperate attempt to save his mistress.

The hound didn't stand a chance. After a few desperate lunges, it vanished under the oncoming hooves.

Lilly skidded to a halt, rage written across her childish face. She stretched out her hands and the leading Pict was catapulted backwards off his steed. She thrust her arms forward again and another rider went down. The remaining warriors yelled louder and spurred their horses on - there were far too many in the raiding party for the girl's fledgling magical powers to stop.

Lilly turned to run again, but a wooden axe came hurtling through the air and embedded itself in her back. She fell forward onto a patch of gorse, a gout of blood erupting in the air.

With a triumphant whoop, the leading Pict dismounted his horse and advanced towards the dying girl.

He never reached her.

There was a rippling in the air. Ferns and heather curled in on themselves, as if subjected to immense heat. The shimmering path reached the Picts, turning them instantly to black outlines that broke and drifted into the sky.

Morgana stood in the doorway, holding Gorrodin's Grail. She ran to her daughter, still clutching the cup, and knelt beside her. With a shudder, the woman pulled the axe from Lilly's back and placed her hand over the spurting wound. She drank from the cup again, whispering hysterically to herself. The blood pouring between her fingers instantly stopped and, when she removed her hand, her daughter's wound was gone. Lilly's shallow laboured breathing evened out until it became deep and regular.

"Sleep, child," Morgana whispered. "When you awake, you will forget this dreadful thing." She hesitated. "Nor will you remember that I broke my sacred promise to your father and used his Grail."

She clasped, then unclasped, her fingers and a small, glinting object appeared in her hand. She fastened it around her sleeping daughter's neck.

It was a tiny silver whistle on a chain.

"If you are ever in trouble again, my child, blow the whistle and I will come to save you."

She carried her child into the house and closed the door.

Charlie and the monster that was once a woman stood a few feet apart. But Morgana no longer seemed interested in him.

She padded over to the house and peered into the window. Her human self was pressing a cloth to Lilly's head, tears streaming down her cheeks.

Charlie walked up behind her.

"Your son is gone," he said. "And you should be ashamed of what you turned him into."

Morgana stayed silent,

"But you still have a daughter. You made a vow to protect her. Remember now?"

The creature whirled round.

"Do not try to trick me, boy."

"Where's the trick?" Charlie kept a respectful distance. "A thousand years without a mother or father, can you imagine that? You were both her world."

He leaned heavily on his sword.

"Go and find your cup, then. Let the Rath destroy Galhadria. But answer me one question first. *Why*?"

The boy sounded defeated.

"To rule? Over what? For revenge? Against who?"

Morgana stared at him.

"That girl is your heir. You should be fighting *for* her, not trying to kill her."

"Where *isssss* my daughter?" Morgana began to search and Charlie joined her, making sure to stay several feet away. But there was no sign of the girl.

Then they heard the sound of a whistle, so faint Charlie wasn't sure if he imagined it. But Morgana's bat-like ears pricked up and she padded into a thicket of long grass.

Lilly lay on her side, curled into a ball, motionless in a pool of blood. The whistle had dropped from her lifeless hand, for the axe Morgana had thrown through the portal was buried in her back.

"Oh, no. no." Charlie knelt beside his friend, cradling her head in his arms. "Not again."

Morgana shuffled on the spot behind him, looking uncertain. She dropped to all fours and began hunting through the greenery.

When she finally stood, she was holding the Grail.

"I have it," she hissed triumphantly.

"Keep the damned thing." Charlie rocked back and forwards, stroking Lilly's matted hair. "You have all the power you could wish for now. Open a portal and go back to your conquest. Wipe out your foes."

Morgana clutched the cup to her chest like a scolded child.

"Now you can spend eternity reigning over your precious Rath, who know nothing but carnage and primal urges. How much satisfaction will you feel, with nobody left to love or to love you?"

"The cup is not ssssomething humans can resissst," Morgana protested.

"Aw, stop pretending you're a victim. You haven't been human for a long time. The cup is yours to command, not the other way round. It's just a bloody object that has brought nothing but misery to everyone who possessed it."

He picked up the whistle and flung it at her.

"Here's another object. Keep it as a reminder of the monster you've become. Not because of how you look or what you did to the man who adored you. Not because you fell under the spell of the Grail."

He laid Lilly gently down.

"Because your only daughter wasted her last breath blowing it."

"That was a very eloquent sssssspeech," Morgana muttered.

"Eloquence is for liars," Charlie shot back. "You know when someone is telling the truth because it always hurts."

Morgana picked up the silver whistle and stared at it. Then she slid the chain over her misshapen head.

"Move." She hunkered down and pushed the boy out of the way. She held the cup to Lilly's lips and poured some of the liquid into her mouth.

"She's gone, Morgana."

"Lilly is a magical creature, like me. We do not die so easily."

She rolled the girl over, placed taloned hands on her back and began to mutter incantations. An orange lambency spread between her claws and the wound began to close.

"It isssss done," she said, exhausted.

Lilly drew a sharp breath and began coughing.

"My God." Charlie stammered. "You did it."

He couldn't be sure, but the creatures fanged lips seemed to turn up at the corners.

Lilly sat up and spotted Morgana. She gave a cry of terror and raised her hands to ward off the creature. The expression vanished from Morgana's face.

"It's all right!" Charlie grabbed the girl's shoulder. "Your mum saved you."

"Mother?" Lilly asked hopefully. "Is that true?"

"Ssstay here and remain hidden, for you are too weak to move." Morgana reached out for the girl, then quickly withdrew her malformed hand. "We must leave, but Charlie will return for you."

"*What?* You two are mortal enemies!"

"I believe we have come to an… undersssstanding."

She spoke a few words and a portal opened behind them. Morgana nodded at the boy.

"Come with me, child, before my will fails."

"That's it?" Charlie sheathed Excalibur. "Aren't you going to tell Lilly you love her?"

"Sometimes wordsssss are not enough."

Morgana locked eyes with her daughter. The girl started as if she had been slapped. Then she smiled.

"I love you too," she said weakly. "I always did."

Morgana leaned over and whispered in Charlie's ear.

"Before we go, you must know sssomething. My daughter did not blow the whisstle to ssssummon me."

She stood and pulled the boy towards the portal.

"She wanted you."

# Morgana

They arrived back on the battlefield to a scene of utter carnage. Exhausted Galhadrians, men and monsters were trading blows in a sea of mud, neither side willing to give an inch. The air was filled with the screams of wounded and dying.

At the sight of their leader, the Rath let out a triumphant roar, quickly changing to confusion when Charlie emerged from the blue light behind her.

"Where isssss Gorrodin?" Morgana demanded.

One of her minions pointed to a far off knot of battling figures.

"Thank you." She sliced him open with one swipe.

"Oooh, that's harsh." Charlie winced.

Morgana took off, barrelling through her own ranks, cutting and tearing their flesh as she went. Charlie ran alongside.

"Don't harm her," he shouted over and over to his side. "She's with me!"

Within minutes Morgana had reached the Clan, or what was left of them. Arthur and Ganieda were badly hurt, leaning feebly against each other. Shadowjack and Gorrodin had fared no better, blood pouring from multiple wounds. The wizard's head was bowed in pain and the blacksmith was holding him up. A handful of knights had formed a defensive ring around them, but their circle was growing ever smaller.

Charlie sprinted past Morgana, holding up the Great Sword.

"Let her through!" he shrieked. "I command it!"

The knights hesitated, then reluctantly parted, allowing Arthur's son and their worst nightmare passage to their leader.

"Charlie!" Ganieda cried. "You're alive!"

"And I brought reinforcements."

Gorrodin raised his head and his eyes widened.

"I return your talisssman." Morgana held out the cup to him. "And relinquisssssh all claim to it."

The wizard reached out and touched her scaly cheek.

"My darling," he said softly. "This moment is worth all the tortures I have endured."

He took the Grail and drank.

The change was instant. He straightened his back and his eyes blazed with renewed energy.

"Goodbye, husband," Morgana said. "Try to forgive me."

She turned and charged into the Rath, arms whirling, flinging them asunder, jaws fastening on one body after another. As the stunned creatures threw themselves upon her, she vanished into the melee.

"Morgana has changed sides!" Gorrodin's voice carried across the battlefield, loud and clear as a bell.

"Since the Dolorous Stroke was struck against her, the Great Spell is now working for us!"

A wail went up from the Rath.

"One more push and the day is ours," the wizard continued. "Victory is assured."

Arthur's men moved forward with renewed vigour. Broken and disheartened, the Rath turned and fled.

They reached the wall of rubble with the enemy on their heels and attempted to climb it. But they were too late. The Galhadrian army swarmed over them.

Fifteen minutes later, the greatest threat Galhadria had ever known had been annihilated.

Ganieda pulled Charlie into her arms.

"I thought I had lost my son," she whispered. "And my heart was torn asunder. I did not realise just how much I loved you."

"I am ashamed to say, I was the same." Arthur kissed the boy's head. "My joy at finding you knows no bounds."

"Then, may I ask a boon?" Charlie wriggled out from their embrace.

"Anything."

"Please, let's go back to talking normally. It's driving me crazy."

"You got it, kid. Call us mum and dad."

Shadowjack and Arthur were allowed small sips of the Grail to speed their recovery. As a Galhadrian, Ganieda healed quickly. She gave her son another kiss then left, to use what magic she had left to aid the injured. Arthur went with her.

Gorrodin approached the boy warily, a sorrowful look on his face.

"Where is my daughter?" he asked. "Is she…?"

"She's alive," Charlie said. "Back at her old home. And when I say back, I mean a thousand years or so. I imagine the Grail knows exactly when."

"How did…"

"Maybe later, eh?"

"I shall use my cup to fetch her immediately." The wizard beamed. "A thousand thanks to you."

He opened a portal and vanished.

Charlie looked around. Bodies were strewn in every direction and the ground was a red pool of gore. Moans and cries drifted through the air and, now and then, a hand was raised pleadingly.

"So this is war." The boy sighed. "What a bloody waste."

He stepped gingerly over corpses until he reached the armoured car.

"You can come out now, Peazle," he shouted, clattering the handle of Excalibur against the metal side. "It's all over."

The hatch opened and Peazle crawled out.

"Did we win?"

"As a matter of fact, we did." Charlie helped him to his feet. "I'll explain later."

"Excellent!" the boy straightened his bowler and took in the scene at a glance.

"By my oath." His face fell. "Is this all that is left of our army?"

"Could have been worse."

"Where is Duncan?"

"I don't know. You should go look for him."

"I'm on my way." Peazle gave a half-hearted grin. "He will be fine, I'm sure."

Charlie avoided his hopeful stare.

"That fellow is imperishable, eh?" Peazle's voice cracked. "Isn't that right?"

"I have to go."

Charlie made his way back to the portal, just as Gorrodin emerged, Lilly leaning on his arm. She hugged Charlie and kissed his cheek.

"Where is my mother?"

"She went this way." Charlie led them across the battlefield towards the wall of rubble. The Rath were so thick on the ground, it was impossible to proceed without stepping on them.

They found Morgana leaning against a rock, half-buried under the creatures she had once commanded. She was covered in lacerations and bite marks, her breathing coming in ragged bursts.

Charlie helped them pull the bodies off, then Gorrodin and Lilly knelt beside the creature.

"You saved us, my darling." Gorrodin cried freely while Lilly squeezed what was left of her mother's mangled hand. Morgana's eyes fluttered open.

"Daughter," she groaned. "I am ssssorry."

"Please don't die," Lilly wept. "We can be together at last."

"I shall use the Grail." Gorrodin yanked the cup from his cloak. "All is not lost."

"Do not usssse that thing on me!" Morgana pushed him away. "You were always too hopeful, husband. Do you never learn from your misssstakes?"

"Of course." Gorrodin nodded.

"Use my fate as a lesson, I beg you." Morgana's eyelids closed. "And please do not think too harshly of me. I tried."

She let out a long breath and passed away.

Charlie left Lilly and Gorrodin to their grieving and went to help his mother tend the injured.


Caleb finally arrived with a ragtag army made up of men and women from the lands surrounding Galhadria. But the battle was long over.

Instead, Arthur requested they help bury the bodies. So they toiled for days, side by side. Gorrodin and Ganieda, restored to full strength, used magic to pile rocks over the remains of the enemy. Then they fashion the remains of the Great Wall into a giant monument. It was a simple design, tall and unadorned. Written at the bottom was an equally plain inscription.

**Here Lie Those Who Fell Defending Their Homes And Families Against the Rath.**

Beyond that was a sea of white crosses, each with a name carved on it. The Galhadrians were still making their way back and would mourn fathers, mothers, uncles, aunts, sisters and brothers when they arrived.

But, before that, the Clan held a private ceremony.

Arthur, Ganieda, Gorrodin, Lilly, Caleb, Shadowjack, Peazle and Charlie stood over a row of graves.

Ganieda stepped forwards.

"You had no stake in this battle, Walter Archer," she said. "Yet you gave your life. On earth, nobody will know what you have done. But, from this day forward, the plain will be known as Archer's Rest. Proof, if it were needed, that some humans are decent to their very core."

"Farewell, sweetheart." Gorrodin placed a wreath on the second mound. "I will never know what torment you suffered. But you overcame it. I loved you and always will."

"Goodbye, mother." Lilly pushed her silver whistle into the earth. "I called and you came."

She began to cry and Gorrodin wrapped her in the folds of his cloak.

Arthur motioned Caleb forwards, but the man shook his head.

"I would give worlds to have more time with my brother but, truth be told, I barely knew him."

He glanced at Peazle.

"His best friend should speak."

"Really?"

"I think it fitting."

Peazle took a huge breath.

"I have always wanting to be a man of learning," he said. "Spent decades acquiring knowledge."

He plunged Duncan's sword into the grave.

"You taught me more than any book could, Duncan Macphail. How to be a good person."

His voice broke.

"I would trade everything I know if I could have you back."

His legs gave way and he sank to his knees, sobbing.

Arthur laid a hand on his shoulder.

"It's Sir Duncan," he said. "King's Champion and Knight of the Round Table."

# Camelot

Arthur's official coronation was a subdued affair, for Galhadria was still lamenting its losses. Even so, the main hall was packed with grateful subjects lining the walls. The human who had suddenly appeared to snatch victory from the jaws of defeat was fast becoming a legend once more.

At Arthur's side sat Queen Ganieda, radiant in white and gold, while Gorrodin stood behind the throne. Once again, he had used sorcery to send his king's message to the crowds thronging outside.

"Castle Alclud is no more," Arthur stood. "From now on, it will be called Camelot. Gorrodin will be my trusted advisor, as he was in happier times."

The wizard nodded solemnly.

He clenched his fist, and an enormous object began to solidify in the centre of the room. Everyone moved back, talking in hushed whispers.

It was a round table, encircled by high backed wooden seats.

"Will my knights take their places?" Arthur asked.

Thirty men stepped forwards, all that was left of the 500 who had gone into battle. Caleb went to join them, but Ganieda waved him back.

193

*Not yet*, she whispered.

Her husband addressed his subjects.

"I understand that many of you who fought with me have families to return to. Those who do not, however, are welcome to join."

Fifty or so Galhadrians took seats, smiling broadly.

"There are still many empty places," Arthur said. "They will eventually be filled by those who have proved brave and true. Not just humans and Galhadrians but those of Alabarra, Monshorn and the Wooded Lands - or anywhere else, for that matter."

There was a shocked silence from those in attendance. Then a cheer went up.

"Arthur! Arthur!"

The king waved for them to be silent.

"I have thought long on this and decided I cannot lead them. My job is to stay here and ensure peace and prosperity in Galhadria."

He beckoned to Charlie.

The boy walked over, casting a surprised glance at his companions. He knelt in front of his king, holding up Excalibur.

Arthur took it and placed the blade gently on the boy's shoulders.

"Arise, Sir Charlie. Commander of my forces and Guardian of the Great Sword."

The cheering grew louder as the boy stood and took back the weapon.

"I will need a second in command," he said in a loud, clear voice. "Therefore, I choose Sir Galahad. Or Caleb, as he prefers to be called."

Caleb looked stunned. Then he took his seat at the round table.

"Now it is time to celebrate," Arthur said. "We have all lost people we loved and will grieve for them to-morrow. Tonight we celebrate them with music and dance, as is our way. For we are all Galhadrians now."

The wooden doors burst open and men entered, bringing food and wine.

"Do we have bards here to sing us songs?"

A dozen hands went up.

"Come forwards and play," Arthur said. "However, tomorrow, I have a task for you."

"What do you wish, my liege?" one asked.

"Together, you will write a ballad about Math and Jack Thane. How they sacrificed themselves that we might live."

"We will pen the most beautiful tune this land has ever heard, with words to match."

"Please do." Arthur smiled sadly. "Jack Thane would have liked that."


The dancing and merriment went on long into the night. Halfway through, Arthur and Ganieda retired to their chambers, motioning for what was left of the Clan to follow.

The king and queen sat on their four-poster bed, while the others lounged on huge, embroidered cushions.

Now that they were alone, Arthur and Ganieda lapsed back into the way they had talked on earth.

"God, I'm pooped," Arthur said. "I never got this tired jumping around in spangly tights."

"I knew you missed it," Ganieda grinned. "You could always introduce sequins as a fashion statement. You're all the rage, right now."

"I'll pass." Arthur lay back on the bed and rolled over. "You can take over while I have a snooze."

"Get up off your lazy butt." Ganieda gave it a slap. "This is important."

"Suppose." Arthur sat up again. "We have a few urgent matters to discuss."

"You have a choice, Lord Peazle," Ganieda pointed at him.

"Did you say, *Lord* Peazle?"

"Don't get all flustered. You deserve it."

"I locked myself in an armoured car while everyone else was fighting. I'll never forgive myself for that."

"It just proves how smart you are." Ganieda shrugged. "You are welcome to become our chief advisor, along with Gorrodin."

"Free library pass forever." Charlie nudged him.

"You said I have a choice."

"Or you can return to the world of men and keep an eye on them." Ganieda grew serious. "You were right, as usual. They have a different kind of magic and, someday, *they* will be Galhadria's greatest threat."

"I presume that's what you really want me to do."

"You'll be able to drink as much Coke and coffee as you like," Arthur cajoled. "Ever have a deep-fried Mars Bar?"

"You had me at Coke." Peazle saluted. "I accept."

"May I go with him?" Shadowjack asked. "I've become very partial to Prawn Cocktail crisps, and skinny boy here will probably need some protecting."

"Of course."

"I shall spend some time with my father," Lilly said. "Then I will go too."

"Are you sure, daughter?" Gorrodin's face fell.

"The truth is, I miss the place. I belong to two worlds and, finally, I am contented with that." She gave her father a hug. "We will return often and tell you of our adventures."

"At great length," Peazle added.

"I shall look forward to each reunion." The wizard kissed Lilly's curls.

"Will you come, Charlie?" the girl asked hesitantly.

"I'm the King's Commander," Charlie shook his head. "I suppose I have commanding to do."

"And your mum has pointed out that mankind is our greatest threat," Lilly persisted. "You might want to help us watch their movements. I'm sure Caleb can manage to keep a few rogue trolls, dwarves and giants in line."

She lowered her eyes.

"I miss Duncan terribly, but he was a friend. To be honest, I have grown to love you."

"Holy smoke." Charlie blushed from head to foot. "You probably guessed I feel the same way."

"Wouldn't have asked otherwise." Lilly winked at him. "I've got my pride, you know."

"Do what your heart dictates, son." Arthur glanced at his wife. "Love is the engine that drives us all."

"My heart soars to hear you say that," Charlie took Lilly's hands. "But my father is wrong. Doing the right thing is what always drove him, and I can ask no less of myself."

"Now, I love you even more. But please stop talking like someone's granddad. It's freaking me out."

Charlie chuckled.

"OK. I got a task to complete. Then wild horses couldn't keep us apart."

"And what is that?"

"I'll take my men to scour every kingdom we know, offering the hand of friendship. Then beyond, to places we have never been. Galhadria's time of isolation is over."

"He is wiser than his years, my liege." Gorrodin smiled approvingly. "And courageous with it."

"Courage is a choice," Charlie said. "It's time to explore. Embrace other cultures and forge alliances. It's time to belong."

He kissed Lilly on the lips.

"I'll be with you someday soon. For now, I've got to take on the task my dad started."

He raised Excalibur and saluted his king.

"To be the Knight With 1,000 Eyes."

**END**

# ABOUT THE AUTHOR

Jan-Andrew Henderson (J.A. Henderson) is the author of 32 children's, teen, YA, adult and non-fiction books. Published in the UK, USA, Australia, Canada, Germany and the Czech Republic, he has been shortlisted for thirteen literary awards and is the winner of the Doncaster Book Prize and the Royal Mail Award.

Subscribe to his website for regular free books, stories, news and advice.

www.janandrewhenderson.com

Lightning Source UK Ltd.
Milton Keynes UK
UKHW010630281221
396285UK00001B/274